DISTANT RUMORS

10 SHORT STORIES

WILLIAM GENSBURGER

B&P BOOKS

Distant Rumors: 10 Short Stories by William Gensburger

Published by B&P Books

First printing: June 2019

Revised edition: March 2023

This edition: Updated with new stories August 2023

ISBN: 978-1-737986270

CONTENTS

CHAPTER ONE
THE FIRST AND FINAL THING

"But man is not made for defeat. A man can be destroyed but not defeated." ~ Ernest Hemingway

DAMN THE FACT that he was six months past due, and damn the fact that he had no one to bitch to, Simon Pratt didn't care anymore.

As he sat on a giant rock atop the mountains somewhere in southern Idaho, midway towards Salt Lake City, he realized he didn't even know the area's name because he had no map, never figuring he would need one.

He took a swig of water from the World War Two

canteen he had brought with him—one of the few things from his father's camping kit that he had brought to this paradise of emptiness.

And, aside from an open fisherman's vest he had purchased from Cabelas a few months earlier, which he wore with army shorts and some hiking boots, he wore nothing else. He had left it all behind.

Six bloody months late. This was him swearing to himself, no words, just the stabbing thoughts that could have had words except for their pointlessness of them.

He'd dropped about forty pounds out here, belly fat replaced by sinewed muscle, workable muscle, not the fancy six-pack abs you would see in men's magazines. He'd earned the muscle, a combination of climbing the mountains, living off the land, and a diet rich in nuts and berries with only the meat he killed himself, which wasn't very often since he was a lousy shot. And this was made worse by the crappy bow and arrow he had built after a few weeks in the bush; shooting the thing wasn't a skill—it was blind luck.

But then, so too, was the fact that six months later he was checking out the range, not just living a fully natural life, but a pain-free one.

He had learned a few survival skills from his father; the two used to camp in these mountains in his youth, and his father would teach him how to find and prepare the many edible plants. He remembered some of that, forgot a lot of it, and relearned some along with new tricks. And thankfully, his father had an old straight blade in the kit that he used for shaving, remembering the old man shaving at the river's edge after using a crushed-up plant for lubrication. Without that, Pratt would have looked the wild bushman part with a full beard. He much preferred a smooth face.

"Damn you, Doctor Mark Peterson," he shouted out. "Damn doctors who can look you in the eye and tell you your life is ending. 'Nothing we can do. Your lab tests confirmed that it's now about the quality of the remaining time you have. We figure a week or two, tops.' Damn you, Doctor Mark Peterson," he shouted again, then defiantly thrust a middle finger to the sky as though the doctor would get that message.

Pratt had given away almost ninety million dollars once the tests returned. He'd have no use for it; he figured the rich lifestyle and rich food had created the disease. Likewise, he did not want to financially burden those he would be leaving behind; an estranged son, Marcus he had been too busy to spend time with, and an ex-wife Janice, who had put up with him for years before she realized she couldn't stand it anymore. He left them well off, with no explanations in the will other than the fact he was on a "Walkabout," a term he learned from the Australian Aboriginals from some movie whose name he could no longer recall. He knew there were Dingoes in there somewhere.

Old Aboriginals wouldn't wait for their death passively; they would go out into the desert to die, releasing their loved ones of the burden. Clean. Neat. And he had always wanted to be more of an outdoorsman than his rich life had allowed. He had few skills in that regard, at least he didn't six months earlier when he drove his car to the base of the trail park of the mountain and walked head-first into the trail with only the canteen, a pocket knife his father had given him, a few memories of camping with his dad, and a paperback novel: "Islands in The Stream" by Ernest Hemingway. He liked Hemingway, a rugged man's man with a great way with words in short, easy-to-chew sentences.

In the car, he had left a note. It read: "Gone for a walk. Won't be back. ~Simon Pratt."

He thought Hemingway would have approved of that, but Hemingway had his booze and his shotgun and had used both, while Pratt had nothing, expecting he would be the dinner for a mountain lion in short order.

In hindsight, he would have brought some booze, at least something to enjoy. On the other hand, the total change of life had been welcoming, embracing, and sustaining in more ways than the fact that he was still breathing. It had cured him.

His mind was clear and sharp. It had no tether to the

business world of before; the false friendships and slap-on-the-back accolades of conquests that involved digital numbers with no blood. The housekeeper, Sylvia, an illegal from Guatemala, bought the groceries, did the laundry, and cleaned the house. He left her some money, at least enough to afford a good immigration lawyer. He never needed to go to the fridge, never washed the dinner dishes, never fed the fat fish in the oversized, pretentious tank that caged them. He felt bad for the fish.

After leaving it all behind him, he only had to consider his next meal, and learn the signs of the animals in the woods with him, especially the ones that would eat him given a chance. He figured out that humans had reduced those to so few in number he had a better chance of running into an overweight duke out here than a mountain lion. To date, he had encountered neither.

Tomorrow I will go down there, he mentally announced, pointing at the ravine below. There would be good pickings there, fruits, berries, certainly something slow that would meet the arrow despite his lack of skill.

The sun was setting, and he watched the sky turn to fire before fading ever so slowly, the streaks thinning and a drab grey settling in. It was warm enough to sleep here—he wouldn't need a blanket or fire. This was his nightly routine; an early night and an early rise. There was something pure about it all.

And as consciousness left him, for the briefest of

moments, he thought how death must be like this. *Perhaps I have already died*, he pondered.

Then, before he knew it, daybreak brought a fresh breeze and a mass of thick puffy clouds that seemed to have been painted on the sky. He'd only seen clouds like this in Idaho, a rapid, dramatic unfolding of the sky in minutes, from this pastoral scene to vapid lightning flashes with the occasional deep thunder rumble, only to clear back to a cloudless sky within a half hour. He thought of the old saying: "If you don't like the weather, wait five minutes."

He'd be safer in the ravine and quickly made haste, watching, with his new insight, the huge bolts that seemed to dance across the entire face of the sky at once. Even the raindrops were huge, big dollops of water that smashed into him.

As he walked, he talked, both parts of a conversation, as though he was not alone.

"Poor and healthy or rich and dying?" he asked.

"Damn crazy choice," he answered. "How 'bout healthy and rich?"

"Nah, screw the bastards. That place is a sucker trap. Work your balls off, and for what? Everyone is two-faced. Corporate greed has poisoned everything. No one has a purpose, anymore; they just stare at those dumb smartphones."

"Yeah, that's harsh, mate. I know. But it is true. I'm

better off alone and able to appreciate the real world, not the pretend world. Who invented the necktie and business suit?"

"It's prison wear."

He made good time down the side of the hill. Above, the lightning continued: an endless light show without sound, not unusual for Idaho. To his right, he caught a glimpse of a deer ducking into the trees. As he came upon a stream, he followed its path, noting its increase in size until, after some time, it had widened significantly into a river. Once the storm passed, he could fashion a fishing line—there was bound to be something in there, perhaps even some trout.

It was a dilemma to him whether to be pissed at the doctor or thankful that whatever had plagued him had resolved itself. He could, if he chose, go back to the world and reclaim his life, even if it was too late to reclaim the money he had disbursed through his demise. And yet those people were dead to him now, memories of someone else's life, and worse, people who might well be unhappy to see him alive after all this time. He had effectively severed all ties with everyone.

Likewise, he could go elsewhere, and start over. He wasn't that old, and was certainly fit. He could remarry, and make a new life in a place he had yet to see. Strangely the thought held little appeal at this time. He did not need anyone. His day was full. The richness of the world around him bled out any thoughts of civilization just beyond the next few ridges. In fact, the only reminder of an actual living world were the aircraft thirty-thousand feet above, contrails, and a quiet, pulsing of the engines as they passed him by, oblivious to his existence.

"What's a man to do?" he asked. He stopped and looked up. The sky had lightened. The clouds were dissipating, and blue was creeping back in.

He found a rock by the river, removed his clothes, grabbed his canteen, then ventured into the shallower side, up to his chest, filling his canteen first and then tossing it toward his clothes.

The water tugged at him, the cold biting at his more sensitive parts. He rubbed his hands over his body as though he were in a luxury bathtub at some pricey hotel, like the ones where he had stayed numerous times before in that other life. Of course, then, he would have had a cocktail by the edge of the tub, lying back and watching some sporting event on the big screen mounted on the opposing wall.

Here, there was just his hands—a thorough water wash. He leaned down to grab a handful of the mud below him and used it to exfoliate. It felt soothing. The rays of sunshine now covered him. The sky was, once again, totally clear.

"Paradise," he said aloud, closing his eyes and facing the sunlight. "Bloody paradise."

"I wouldn't go that far," a woman's voice said from the shore, breaking his spell. He opened his eyes, and focused on her.

"Bloody hell," he said. "Who are you?"

She teetered, grabbed the closest boulder, and leaned into it. Her clothes were torn, and her hair was a tangled mess. She was bleeding from a small gash on one leg.

"You're hurt," he said, striding out of the water toward his clothes. The woman looked at him, then turned away. Even injured, it wasn't every day that she saw a naked man in peak physical form striding out of a river like a God.

Simon pulled on his shorts, then moved toward her, studying the gash on her leg.

"Does it hurt much?" he asked. She nodded, then looked up at him, moving her hair aside with the back of her hand. "How'd you get here?"

"Plane," she said, her voice raw. "Do you have something to drink?"

"Water," he answered, retrieving his canteen and handing it to her. "Plane? Crash?"

She nodded.

"The storm?"

She shook her head. "Before," she said, gulping the water.

"Are you alone?" Simon asked.

"Thank you," she said, handing him the canteen. "My pilot died in the crash. He had lost his bearings."

He returned to his shirt, ripped it into a few long strips as best he could, then went back to the river and soaked one strip in the water. He grabbed a handful of mud by the edge where the water was lapping and placed it inside the strip, closing it off with a knot at each end. Then, returning to her, he first poured the water from the canteen across the wound, then placed the mudpack over it, tying it to her leg with the additional strips. "Too tight?"

"It's fine. Thank you." She stood up and put some weight on it, but it still hurt too much.

"They're gonna come looking for you," he told her. "Probably won't make progress until the morning. We'll have to camp here tonight. You can't go anywhere."

He helped her walk to a clearing a short distance away, beneath a rush of trees that would serve them well. Then helped her to sit against a fallen log. "I'll get a fire started and try to get us some food."

"What's your name," she asked.

"Simon," he told her.

"I'm Annie. Thank you for helping me."

"Nice to meet you, Annie," he said. "You're the first person I've seen in half a year."

"Are you lost?" she asked. And he started to laugh.

"You could say that," he said, then went off to gather wood and anything he could find to eat. First, he returned with some broken twigs and small branches, then larger ones that would burn more slowly, setting them up for a small campfire. Then he used a vine to trap a stick and friction-lit the fire. He had done it many times but never on the spot, pulling raw items from the floor as needed. The fire was not cooperating. Annie watched him for a moment, then reached into her pocket and withdrew a lighter and a pack of cigarettes. She lit a cigarette, inhaled deeply, then extended the lighter to him.

"Will this help?"

Simon stared at her, nodded, and took the lighter, igniting the small mound of kindling and adding a few smaller branches. He handed the lighter back.

"Thanks. Those things will kill you," he added, motioning to the cigarette.

"Yes," she said. "But it almost didn't."

"I'll get something to eat. Be back in a bit." He handed her the canteen.

Further up, he spotted some familiar plants that he had eaten before. Wild ginger, a strong bite, but totally healthy. And Camas, a medicinal plant with blue leaves and bright yellow stamen. And nestled beneath an outgrowth, wild strawberry, its leaves reminding him of poison oak, but greener, softer. He had discovered those by accident shortly after he departed. Cattails were abundant, and he bent and pulled up a handful of the roots. He would have to clean and crush them, allowing them to soak in the water until their starch settled to the bottom. Since he had no pot, he would make one out of the earth, smooth it and use that to make his dinner. Camas would have to bake in the fire and, given how short amount of time he planned to cook, would likely be difficult to stomach. Still, it was better than nothing. Elk Thistle, a prickly-looking shrub with purple hues, was also common, and he knew it as a tasty treat. He would grab the top of the plant and bend it, seeking out the point where it began to stiffen before breaking it off. These stems had a sweet, delicate taste.

In the river, where it hollowed into a calm, he could see small fish gathering. How nice it would be to swoop in and scoop them up, he thought, but he knew that would not happen. Instead, his guest would have to be content with the bounty he had just collected.

He'd been gone a short time, but the woman was happy to see him return. He dropped the items he had collected, then went to check on her.

"I was getting worried," she said.

"No need," he told her. "I've had much practice out here. But let me ask you—where did your plane crash? Is it a short distance from here?"

She pointed to the east, behind the small mountain across the other side of the river. "I walked under an hour until I had no more strength," she said. "Why?"

“The pilot,” he said. “We should be sure that he did not survive.”

“He didn’t. I checked.” She lit another cigarette and watched as he used a rock to hollow out the ground enough to form a slightly concave shape. Then, finding another flatter rock, he crushed up the ginger and Camus, adding a bit of water, then scooping the gristly half-paste with a leaf and handed it to her along with the canteen.

"It'll taste like shit, but it'll help you heal."

Carefully she took it, and sniffed at it. "Ginger?"

"Yeah. And if you eat it fast, I'll even give you a wild strawberry to chase the taste."

Obediently, she scraped it off the leaf with her teeth, wincing at the potency and the sting against her tongue. She swallowed it with a swig of water from the canteen, and when she was done, he was standing before her holding two small wild strawberries.

"Imagine that," she said with a smile, taking one and popping it in her mouth, overcome with the pleasure of the sweetness. "Aren't you a treasure?"

He continued with their dinner, dropping the handful of cattails into the small earth bowl shape he had smoothed out. He crushed them up and poured the rest of the canteen into the bowl. There wasn't enough water, so he went to refill at the river, making ten trips to compensate for the water draining away into the soil, but enough to release the starches from the cattails.

All the while, she watched him, not saying a word. She looked at the tight, sinewy muscles of his arms and legs, the fine hairs that had been bleached by his exposure to the sun. She studied the lines on his face, well-earned creases that looked less a sign of age than of style. His eyes seemed a deeper blue than she was used to, offset by the well-tanned skin and white teeth. As he leaned over to stir his concoction, she watched the muscles of his back ripple. The man had no fat on him, not something she could claim, as she looked down at the exposed part of her leg around the wound. But what was he doing here?

He added some of the other plants, grinding them, crushing them, and the flowers simply rubbing them apart in his hands, allowing the bits to fall into his earth soup mix. He stirred it together with his hands until she noticed that it looked like a soft dough, sticky, pliable. She wondered how it would taste.

He stood, rubbing the excess bits from his hands, and noticed her staring at him. Her look was different. Softer.

"What?" he asked. She smiled. "What?" he asked again. "Is something wrong?"

She shook her head. "I just wanted to say thank you for saving me. Without you, who knows what would have happened to me."

True enough, he thought. With her leg wound, she would make tempting prey to whatever was lurking around. Bears. Coyotes. Wolves. Despite the remoteness he felt, he knew they were out there with him, and had heard them periodically, especially after they had scored a meal.

"You're welcome," he replied. "You can thank my father for a few survival skills when I was a kid. Besides, it's . . . nice to have some company for a change." He grabbed a few larger leaves from the tree next to them and flattened them on the ground. Then, carefully, he pulled at the dough mix and rolled it into many bite-sized bits, placing them neatly on the leaves. He handed one leaf to her. "No napkins, I'm afraid."

She looked at it dubiously. "Do I savor it or swallow it?"

He laughed. "Honestly, I don't know. Probably a bit of both. The sticky part is starch, so it will be bland, but the rest will have an interesting taste. It's all good for you."

"Ah," she said, picking up one of the balls. "Organic. You'd pay a fortune for this in the store." She plopped it in her mouth, held it on her tongue for a moment, then chewed into it. "Not bad," she told him. "It tastes like overcooked rice with some green vegetables. Could use salt, but not bad at all."

Satisfied that he had done well, Simon took his leaf and moved closer to her, sitting and eating.

"So what is your story?" she asked after a time. "How did you come to live in the bush?"

"Well," he began,"I'm dead." Then seeing the quizzical

look on her face he added, "Well, I'm supposed to be, anyway."

"You look very well for a dead man," she said. "You are perhaps one of the fittest men I know."

"Well, that's the rub, you see. They told me I was terminal. Gave me a few weeks, tops. No treatment would work, just delay, and the last thing I wanted was to die a skeleton, everyone treating me like someone who is going to die. Not to mention the burden and the cost. What a way to go out. So I decided to do it my way. My grandfather was from Australia and told me how the old Aboriginals would leave and go walk the desert to die rather than be a burden on their family. Sounded like a terrific idea."

"Only you didn't die," she added for him.

"Only I didn't die," he repeated, raising his eyebrows to express his incredulity at the event."In fact, I've never felt better, never slept better, and never had so much energy."

She finished the last dinner balls and used the leaf to wipe the sticky starch off her fingers.

"So you can go home?"

"I suppose."

She studied his face. "You don't want to?"

"It's not that . . . ."

"I don't understand," she said. "Even though you rescued me, I want to go home, back to the life I had before I fell out of the sky."

"People waiting for you?" he asked.

"Perhaps," she said, lighting another cigarette and inhaling deeply.

"You better hope they rescue you before you run out of those things," he said. "You might have to resort to smoking leaves."

She laughed, a deeper throaty laugh that sounded genuine. Not that he approved of the smoking—he couldn't imagine doing such a thing.

"I hope so, too," she told him. "But to answer your question, there is no one in particular who would be waiting for me. It's just the familiarity of the world I know, warts and all. How about you? Surely you had a wife who loved you and children who miss you?"

"I had an ex-wife who is probably very happy having received a decent inheritance. And I had a son who was closer to his mother's boyfriend than he was to me." He paused and looked at the sky. It was already getting darker. "The thing is that to them, I have been dead for over a half year. Dead, settled, assets divvied up. I am no longer a part of the living world. I have no more social security number, no more driver's license, no bank accounts, and no credit cards. I am a ghost. Everything that made me Simon Pratt no longer exists, legally. I have no home. I wander the countryside and enjoy the beauty of nature that I never paid any attention to before, and revel in the sunrises and sunsets. I talk to myself, the trees, the birds, and the fish."

"But, do they talk back?" Annie asked him, their eyes locking for the longest of moments before he shook his head. "I'm so sorry," she said.

"It is how it is," he said. "Being here makes me realize that the world we accept as real is just a series of choices and events. We stop questioning the validity of it. We work, make money, play games, have sex, drink too much, laugh too little, and watch those older than us wither and die. And we take their place in this cycle, never stopping long enough to ask why we spend our entire life working a job that serves only to pay bills."

"That is the way society operates," Annie said wistfully. "How sad to have to always think about the end of life or a lack of meaning."

"But there is plenty of meaning," he told her, waving his hands around him. "This. This is the real world. It is not a human world with small boxes in which we live. It is life before we came along. It will be life long after we are gone, probably."

She let off a throaty laugh, and he caught, in her reaction, his over-seriousness.

"Sorry," he said. "I ramble."

"Not at all," she told him. "It is very charming. And very insightful."

"I'll bet you say that to all the guys you get stranded with!"

She laughed again, pushed herself upright, and extended a hand for him to help her up. "Let's go for a walk."

"A walk? You mean a hobble?"

She nodded as he grabbed hold of her. "Yes. A hobble. I will rely on your strength."

Already the sky was darkening, and Simon knew that they would have to make camp here for the night. He had left his gear, what little he had, at his main camp. Hopefully, they could reach it in the morning.

"So, Dorothy. What do you do when you're not in Oz?" he asked her.

"I edit books for a publishing company. And I take photographs for some magazines."

"That sounds interesting," he said, showing no expression. But she looked directly at him and smiled.

"You are a very good liar, Sir Galahad."

"Am I now?" he asked.

At the river edge, he helped her to sit on a large tree trunk that had fallen, part of its bulk resting in the water. The evening sounds permeated everything; the birds chattering, flying back and forth, the stillness in the air, and the serenity of the river flow. "So peaceful," she said.

"How it should be," he replied. "We're going to have to

camp out tonight. In a bit, I'll get the fire built up and see about some kind of bedding.

"You'll have to sleep on the couch," she said with a chuckle. "I'm not that kind of woman, you know."

"I had no doubts of that, Annie. Besides, as a gentleman, of course, I would take the couch."

She ran her hand against the back of his head affectionately.

"Of course, I have to find the bloody couch first," he told her.

Later, after he had made her a mound to lie on from leaves and thin bark he had scrounged along the river, and as he tended the fire, bringing it to a solid roar without needing her lighter this time, he caught her watching him again. She smiled serenely as their eyes met.

"When I was a little girl," she began,"my father would camp with me in our backyard. We lived in Belgium back then, before we came to this country. He would pile the blankets into a mound like this, and we would lie together and stare at the stars. It's funny that I think of that now," she said, reaching for her pack of cigarettes and holding it up. The pack was empty. "I'm done for," she said, crumpling it into a ball and tossing it in the fire from where she sat. "I guess I am officially a non-smoker now."

"That's a good thing," he said. "I hope it won't be too hard to quit."

"It is what it is," she said. "My father would always point to a star—I can't recall which star—and he would tell me that perhaps someone was there, like us, a father and daughter, just sharing one moment together, looking at our world, and thinking the same thing."

"You were close?"

"Very. He was my everything when I was a girl. I loved everything about him, his voice, the way he walked. He smoked a pipe, and the smell of tobacco on his jackets; I still think of him whenever someone is smoking a pipe."

"Is he still alive?"

"I was thirteen. He died a week after what I shared. I was devastated."

"I'm sorry."

"Me too."

"You were lucky. He knew how you felt about him. My son and I . . . well, I guess I could have been a better father. And he could have been a better son. He decided some years ago that I was wrong, did not understand him, and confined him. He wanted to be free of me, to make his own choices, is what he said. After that, we would only text message. He never wanted to come by for dinner or just visit. Holidays and birthdays, just a text message. Happy dad day, not even a bloody capital 'D'."

"I'm sorry," she said.

"He found his mother's new boyfriend to be more . . . fun. They would do things together and hang out together. I was still living the corporate life, always scheduled, making lots of money, but not much else." He stopped, and looked up at the stars that had begun to appear. "I was good at it. It seems such a waste, now." He looked back at her. "When I started to feel quite ill, I kept it to myself. That wasn't hard to do. My wife had left. My son had left. I wasn't seeing anyone. I had declined friends' requests to dinners and events and kept to myself. I thought I had the flu or some such thing; that it would pass. But it didn't. Finally, I went to the doctor and found out I only had a few weeks left."

"Did you tell your son? Your wife?"

He shook his head. "The last thing I wanted was sympathy. For better or worse, no matter what happened from that point until the end, it would not change the ending. Why make it worse? For them. I recorded my will on DVD at my lawyers, so there would be no contesting, arranged the personal effects I wanted my son to have if he decided to keep them, and left him a letter letting him know that I loved him very much and hoped he would not feel any guilt because I wouldn't want him to. And left them both a lot of money, enough that they would never worry about money the rest of their life."

"Wow," she said. "I cannot imagine . . . ."

"I took the canteen—it was my father's from the war,

my fishing jacket, and my old paperback book, and drove to the base of a trail close to my house. Left the keys inside and a note. And then started to climb. I figured I would last a day before I got attacked by something. I thought that would be better than getting treated with IV's and doped up on painkillers. And here we are."

"Well, I am very happy that you managed to stay alive," Annie said, "and not because you saved my life; you are a kind man. A very kind man. There are not so many kind men in the world anymore."

"That's very sweet," he said. "Thank you."

"And I am also glad you are not alone anymore."

He looked at her. "For now. In the morning, we should try to get back to my camp. I have a bow and arrow there, and we can get a better idea of how to get you home."

She nodded. "Home," she muttered. "It seems very far away."

"Probably closer than you think. We might also consider backtracking to see if we can find the wreckage of your plane. We might be able to salvage some of it. Where were you going, anyway?"

"Nowhere. It was a birthday gift from a cousin of mine. A scenic trip around the mountains. It was supposed to be an hour or two only."

"When was your birthday?"

"The day I crashed. Good timing, eh?"

"Well, Happy Belated Birthday, Annie. I'm sorry that it was not better."

And then they drifted to sleep, the fire continuing to burn for several more hours. In the distance, not close to them, a coyote began to yap. For whatever reason, the animals that lived in the backwoods seemed oblivious to them.

In the morning, when she opened her eyes, the fire had been rekindled, and a wide leaf filled with berries lay within arms reach.

"Did you sleep well?" he asked her. She nodded, getting to her feet. Her leg felt better, and she stretched it, then leaned over to untie the poultice he had placed there. Exposed, the wound looked good; the swelling had subsided, and she did not feel the pain she had felt the day before.

"Don't overdo it," he advised her, motioning for her to eat.

"I dreamed of flying," she said.

"Better than the reality of the last flight," he said carelessly.

"Indeed." She popped a berry into her mouth and sucked on its sweetness as she stared at Simon, his eyes scanning their surroundings, always scanning.

"Do you think backtracking to the wreckage will help?"

He looked at her for a moment. "You're sure the pilot died?"

She nodded. Looked down. In her mind, she imagined his body being the dinner for the creatures that lived in the woods. She did not wish to see more of that.

"Well, it might make more sense to get you back to civilization and have them send a recovery effort."

She nodded. "Yes, that's what I think, too." She wanted to tell him that at that moment, she felt safe, safer than she had before the flight; certainly less alone than she had felt then. The flight was not just a birthday celebration; it was an escape, well, as much of one as she could muster. What was it about Simon that instilled such trust in her? He had only been in her life one day. One day! It was a reckless thought, but she thought it anyway. A day is enough time to get to know someone.

"We'll cut back through the hills behind us," he explained. "It's just a short incline, and you should be able to manage that. From there, it's all downhill for a few hours." He laughed, a single short laugh that seemed odd.

"What?"

"Nah, nothing."

"Really. What?" She insisted.

"Ironically, it will take us to where my journey started," he explained. "Right at the foot of a hiking trail.

There should be other people around so we can get you help."

She stared at him for a minute. "And you?"

"What about me?"

"Will you come back with me, Simon?"

Their eyes met and held as he thought about what she was saying.

"I can't go back there," he said plainly. "I'm dead to them all. There's nothing left there but old memories and disappointments. I don't think that would be a good thing."

She seemed sad but then shook her head, her hair swaying to one side. "What if we run away together?"

"Now you're talking," he said, but he was not serious, and she knew it. The practicality of starting a new life somewhere else, with someone he had just met, was as insane as his walking away from his old life expecting to die. "Italy," he added, continuing the joke. "We could do one of those boat rides . . . ."

"Gondolas," she said for him. "How lovely that would be. Italy is the city of romance, you know?"

"I thought that was Paris," he said.

She nodded. "Both of them. But I prefer Italy. Have you been?"

He shook his head no.

"A shame. You'd love it. We could wander the countryside—you're already dressed for it—and soak in the sunshine and the right aromas in the air." Her eyes were closed, her face toward the sun, and a smile formed. Simon watched, studied her face, the curves, the way small dimples formed when she smiled like that.

"I don't know any Italian," he said.

"I'll teach you," she countered. He stared at her.

"Really? You speak Italian?"

She tried keeping a straight face but couldn't hold it. "No. But we could learn it together." And she broke out in a hearty laugh that caught him off guard and made him start to laugh as well. She had tears from the laughter, and each time one would look at the other, the laughter renewed, on and on until, finally exhausted, they settled into a muffled laugh, a smile, and then just stared at each other.

"You are filled with surprises," he told her. Their eyes remained locked. He moved closer and gently kissed her on the lips, their eyes still firm. "Where were you all those years ago?"

She smiled at him and ran a finger gently across her lips. "Getting ready for you," she finally said.

"And here we are," he told her, abruptly snapping back to reality, packing up the makeshift campsite. She watched, unsure of what she should say or do. He had a place where no one could come, and you could see it as he moved, carefully arranging things he had come to regard as a habit; motions, actions, senses on alert, a man in the midst of nowhere and yet perfectly in tune with his surroundings. She could only watch.

She considered that a cigarette would be good but then realized she really didn't miss it at all. How easily that crutch had faded away.

Once he had everything packed, secured against a log for his later return, they started along the route he had chosen, walking silently. Once in awhile, he would stop and offer her some water from his flask, which she would take so that she could look at his face and into his eyes. It wasn't so much that she wanted to hear him say something, as much as wanting to say something herself, to continue their earlier conversation, even if in jest.

After another half-hour, she needed to rest. "Stop," she said weakly, and he turned suddenly, realizing that he had pushed her too far. He moved to her side, reached for her arm, and gently helped her to sit on a log to one side.

"I'm sorry," he said. "I pushed you . . . ."

"No . . . just needed a moment to catch my breath," she said with a smile. "I'm not in your kind of shape, ex-smoker and all."

"You're doing great. We can rest here. We're making good time."

He looked around, poked the underbrush, and pulled

up a root that he wiped off. Once it was mostly dirt free, he offered it to her. "Suck on this. It's sweet."

She took it with a smile. "You are so clever with these things." Looking at it first, she put the root end in her mouth and did as he had told her. "Hmmm, it *is* sweet," she said. "It's quite good."

He popped down beside her. "Look about earlier . . . ."

"Shh, you don't have to say anything. It was just a silly fantasy," she said.

"Not so silly, really," he said. "Look, I can't explain it . . . we've just met . . . it's nuts to expect to know someone so quickly . . . ."

"I feel the same," she said, her voice still raspy. "But we're not teenagers. This isn't how it should happen. Is it?"

"If at all," he added.

"If at all."

They fell silent again.

"But . . . you make me laugh," she said, "and I have not laughed like that in a long time. It must mean something."

"It does."

"It does?"

He nodded and let it be just a moment of bliss, like a droplet of rain balancing on a single blade of grass after a storm.

"Shall we move?" He held out a hand and pulled her upright. Staring at her, he was about to say something but the words wouldn't form, so he turned and started to walk again.

They had reached the summit, and before them was a large canyon thick with trees except for a winding path that led the way down. He pointed at it. "My trail," he said. "My God, I never thought I would see it again."

She moved closer, and patted him on the back. "Well, I'm glad you made it, or I would never have met you, and that would have been quite sad."

He looked back and smiled at her, which brought a smile to her face, then he started to laugh.

"What did I do now?" she demanded.

"If you had never met me, you wouldn't have been sad," he explained, and when she heard him say it, she understood the humor and started to laugh.

"You know what I meant," she finally said, then, looking out at the lushness, just shook her head. "It's so beautiful."

"The first and final thing," he said.

"What's that?"

"Hemingway," he said, pausing for a deep breath of the clean air. "The first and final thing you must do in this world is to survive it and not be smashed by it."

"That's lovely," she said. "Hemingway? You like Hemingway?"

Simon nodded. "He kept me sane when I got here. All I had was a pretty worn-out paperback novel he wrote. I guess had he written about this place, it would have been called 'The Old Man and the Mountain . . . .'"

"You're not old. And you did not get smashed." She threw him a smile, and he smiled back.

"Nor you," he replied, setting off down the path. "Watch your step."

They stopped again after the fifth hour of walking. Any small things that were edible along the way he had picked and passed back to her. He didn't need it; he was good for another handful of hours before he'd have to eat. But they wouldn't be out that much longer.

And then she will return to her world, he thought, and I to mine, and in all likelihood, they would never see each other again unless one of them changed their minds; Annie to stay with him, and Simon to take a chance and return to that other world, the one he had loathed and left. The one that had let him down.

Two hours later, the trail broadened, and the trees thinned out. Clearly, this was the start of civilization, broad swaths of grasses with "No Littering" signs here and there. He stopped to take it in, and turned to meet her eyes. "The jungle," he said with a smile. "Gotta watch for predators now." She laughed just a bit and reached for his hand, which he held as they walked on.

A few hundred yards further and they came across a man on a mountain bike. Flagging him to a stop, Simon asked him to call the police, which he did, noting the mile marker of the trail so they could be found. Then the biker left. Simon and Annie sat down on a bench and waited a half hour for the police to arrive.

"Are you ready?" he asked her. She shrugged.

"There are no words . . . ," she said.

"I know," he told her, squeezing her hand. "You are a remarkable woman, Annie. I'm glad that you fell out of the sky." She smiled at that.

"And you are a remarkable man, Simon. You made me feel again." She held his face in her hands, staring into those eyes. "I wish you would come with me."

"I do, too," he said. "But I can't go back there, Annie. I'm dead to them, and they are dead to me. I can't imagine trying to fit back into a world I can barely remember. Leaving it made me live. Had I stayed . . . well, we wouldn't be here. I hope you understand?"

She nodded. "I do."

A patrol car pulled up next to them, and two officers got out, suspicious of the half-naked wild man and the bedraggled woman beside him.

"Officers," Simon began. "This is Annie. Her plane crashed a few days ago in the mountains, and I've brought her home.

"Plane crash? Are you Annie Holsten from Meridian?" one of them asked. She nodded.

"Wow!" the other said. "You're presumed dead. Search party lost the trail. It's been all over the news."

"Well, here she is," Simon said, standing up as though he were about to leave. "Alive and well."

"Who are you?"

"Me?" Simon laughed. "Hell, no one. Just a bloke in the mountains fishing."

"What's your name? I need some ID?"

"Mark," he lied. "Dr. Mark Peterson. I have no ID, I'm afraid. But I'm in the phone book."

"He saved my life," Annie told them. "I'm grateful to him. Please leave him be."

"Look, I'd better get back," Simon said. "Don't want my dinner getting cold."

"You sure you don't need medical help?" one of the officers asked.

"I'm fine," he told them, "but her leg should be looked at. I did the best with what I had—nasty gash."

"Annie, take care of yourself, okay?" He held her close, their eyes locked.

"And you, too. Think of me?"

He nodded, allowed their lips a final kiss, then turned back to the trail and swiftly started the climb back home. Annie and the police officers watched him until he disappeared.

"Bit of an odd one," one of the officers remarked.

"Indeed," Annie said with a smile as they helped her into the car and left for the hospital.

Simon Pratt spat out into the wind as he sat on a giant rock atop the mountains somewhere in southern Idaho, midway towards Salt Lake City. He still didn't even know the name of the area because he had no map never figuring he would need one. But he had sat on this rock half a year earlier when he first left society in order to die a peaceful death. Only then, as he recalled, he had been cursing to the sky, profanities directed at Mark Peterson, the doctor who had sent him home to make his final arrangements. At least Peterson had actually saved a life, even indirectly by Simon's presence when Annie needed him.

"Annie," he said softly to the wind. "I wish I could have said yes. I wish I had met you so many years ago. It would have all been different." But then he remembered his diagnosis and the likelihood he would have died at home in her arms had that life happened, leaving her a widow and grieving.

"It's better to have loved and lost than never having loved at all," he shouted out to the wind. Then, standing, thrust a middle finger to the sky and added: "You, too, Shakespeare," and continued the trek home.

By the time he returned the following evening, the campsite was as he had left it. His few possessions were still snugly wedged under the log, and he pulled them out, arranged his things, and settled in for a long sleep.

It was the big water droplets that woke him a few hours later as a hefty thunderstorm had rolled in. The stars were gone, replaced by an ongoing show of lightning flashes dancing between clouds and to the ground, only the latter releasing an ear-splitting "boom." The lightning silent-symphony kept going, one flash after another, sometimes a series of them illuminating the clouds from inside. He still didn't know how there could be no sound; by its nature thunder was the byproduct of the massive discharge. He ignored the raindrops and stared at the show, hypnotized by the lights. It was incredibly beautiful, one of the things he had always loved about Idaho mountains. A wind rose, warm, enveloping despite the water, and Simon just closed his eyes and allowed it to consume him as he drifted back to sleep.

The next morning, and the next fourteen after that, the sky was clear and blue. Birds were swooping. A few deer crossed the stream ahead of him, oblivious to his presence. He tried to clear his head but found himself thinking of Annie, wondering where she was. She was lost to him. Even if he had changed his mind, he didn't know where to look for her. He pondered this as he got up and muttering to himself, brushed leaves from his body.

"Hi, can you help me. I'm looking for this woman who crashed a little way from here?"

He started foraging for breakfast, remembering the berries that he had found for her. "Stupid, stupid," he said. "Stop thinking about her. She's gone. Get back to your life before she came along. You had it made. It was all so simple then."

But the land seemed less rich, the air too dry. And the days lasted far too long before the darkness swallowed his thoughts once again.

He sat on a fallen limb and pondered what he had learned. Could he go back? He felt certain that when he had left, it was a one-way trip. There was simplicity here, no one to deceive him, no one to let him down. Yes, he had been a lousy father and certainly a lousy husband, all in pursuit of a career. He had been damned good at that. The drinking, the food, getting lost in the haze of the expectations of his stature. He was someone. . . someone with nothing else worth anything. And now, here, he was no one with everything of worth around him. What a waste of a life, he pondered. All those years that could have been better spent.

And then he thought of Annie, yet again.

It was only the sound of a low-flying airplane that snapped his attention back. It was close, and after searching, he spotted it in the distance, circling over one area. He knew they must have found the wreckage of Annie's plane; it seemed the right distance away. He watched it for a while, then decided he should return to his home higher up the mountain. Perhaps when he got there, he could read from Hemingway's novel, and stop his mind from chasing memories he could no longer control.

Turning, he started off, looking back every few minutes to see if the plane was still circling. It wasn't. Now it was heading closer to where he had been. He ducked out of sight, and watched to see what was happening. As it got closer, it started to circle where he had spent the night, getting lower with each pass. He couldn't see who was flying the plane and wondered if it was Annie who had somehow returned looking for him. Should he run out and wave his hands to get her attention? Except she could not land and what would be gained. Their situations were still the same. And so he stayed hidden, waiting for the plane to leave.

Then something dropped from the plane, a small parachute opening behind it. It was a canister swinging with the wind until it hit the ground with a "thud" and split open, spilling its contents out.

The plane circled one final time and then left, quickly

disappearing in the distance from where it had come. He stared after it watching it get smaller.

Simon moved out from the trees and walked back toward the canister. Even though it had broken, its contents were still wrapped in thick plastic bags. There were a handful of bags, and he could see the contents inside. One bag had clothes; shirts, shorts, slacks, socks, shoes, a sport coat, and even underwear, all tightly compressed. Another held some lighters, medical supplies, and a small pocket radio. A third bag had some food items, tins of baked beans mostly, along with a can opener. The last bag he picked up and carefully studied. Inside were a variety of envelopes and a notecard.

He tore open the plastic and pulled out the contents, first opening the notecard. It read:

Dear Simon,

Some things every bushman needs in case a lady in distress should fall from the sky.

But seriously, I have missed you terribly, and I hope that you have missed me too. I think you do.

I've been thinking about our situation. I know you can never live here, and quite frankly, I would be terrible in the bush, as you have discovered already. I know that as far as you are concerned, you are dead to the world.

And so I have come up with a good plan that I hope

you will like. I'm leaving the country. I've put my house up for sale, cashed in my assets, and one way or another, I will live the life I have always dreamed of.

I had to take a few liberties to make all this work properly, you understand, and I want you to know that I have been very careful and called upon a few trusted friends to help make this dream happen.

I know that I am in love with you, and I know that, crazy or not, I want to spend whatever time I have left with you and not without you. If you feel the same way, of course.

And so, my dear Bryan, I hope you give this as much thought as I have. I believe Ernest would agree with me.

If you do feel the way I do, you will know what to do.

Love Annie

"What the hell..." Simon held the card and reread it. "Bryan?" She knew his name. It had to be a joke.

He opened the other envelope, a long plastic sleeve in which he found one airline ticket, one passport, and some cash. The airline ticket was one-way to Naples, Italy, with a Post-It note stuck with the words "Final destination: Positano" written in a woman's handwriting. The flight date was in just three days. But the ticket was made out in the name of Bryan Delano.

"Bryan Delano," he said aloud. "Who the hell is Bryan Delano?"

He was mildly amused but also irritated. It had to be a joke. But the airline ticket looked real.

He glanced down at the bag with the clothes and realized that the sport coat, shirt, slacks, and shoes were traveling clothes. Airplane clothes. But still . . . .

He opened the passport and flipped to the main page, and saw his face staring back. There he was, an older photo before he left—she must have found it Online—but with the name Bryan Delano. He started to laugh, walking around in a small circle clutching the passport and ticket, shaking his head, and just laughing.

This was her solution. Leave the old behind and live again anew. Totally anew. Italy! It was crazy. Insane. Just pack up and leave . . . not that he had anything to really pack up, and he had already left it all behind.

The real question, he told himself, was how he felt about her. It was, he quickly answered, a stupid question. He had no doubts about how he felt. Since she had returned to the world, he had been miserable. Now, this. He was excited, nervous, and determined. Only an idiot would let this woman slip by a second time.

He gathered up the bags and discovered a duffel bag beneath them. Obviously, it was meant to carry everything. She certainly had given it a lot of thought.

First, he would have to go back up the mountain to get

the few things he wanted to bring, the worn-out copy of "Islands in The Stream." He liked Hemingway. He agreed that Hemingway would have approved of his new life in Italy with Annie.

The trip back down to the city—the same route he had recently taken with Annie— he could manage at a faster pace than she could manage. The cash meant a ride to the airport, where he would have enough time to clean up. Would she even recognize him?

With the last of the items in the duffel bag, he zippered it up, noticing yet another note card that fell out at his feet. He picked it up, ripped it open, and read it. He began to laugh, letting the note fall to the ground as he turned and rapidly walked toward home.

The note just read: "Hurry." ■

CHAPTER TWO
THE CAT LIVED

THE CAT DIED on a Saturday morning amidst a blaze of activity designed to save its life. Hooked up to tubes, bandaged, and shaved in crucial areas, the cat awaited execution atop the sterile metal table in one of the examination rooms. Howling dogs could be heard in the background.

It was Jane who called it "execution." The veterinarian had softened such harsh realities to "putting the poor thing out of its misery" or "putting him to sleep." But then the vet had also joked about putting her own husband to sleep and had not intended that to come across as a peaceful transition.

"There could be some spasms after the injection. It may not look pretty. Are you sure you wouldn't rather wait in the outer office while we do this?" she asked.

Jane shook her head. Her husband, Jason, watched from behind. Despite the sadness of the moment, he found himself intrigued by the unfolding event, semi-detached as though he were watching a National Geographic television special or one of those made-for-television movies that were so popular a few years earlier.

He noticed the calmness of the vet, the way her face would contort into a grieved expression without the substance of grief, as though she wanted you to believe that she was killing her own pet rather than yours. He did not feel convinced.

The vet tech attached another tube, one into which fast-acting poison would later be injected. The first shot is only a sedative to calm the animal, he was told. The second one paralyzes the heart. *Ka-boom!*

Robert could envision a future world in which the elderly were dispatched with the same precision and the consoling pre-eulogy of the attending physician "putting the poor thing out of his/her misery."

"It's better this way," the vet said, her eyes offering another rendition of sadness and sympathy as she discharged the contents of the syringe through the tube leading into the cat.

The cat's head, which until this point had been free-moving, slowly dropped to the table, its eyes flickering then glazing over as the lids closed one last time. And that was it.

"Would you like us to take care of his remains?" the vet asked.

"Please," Jason said, clearing his throat and answering before Jane could argue a case for burying it in the backyard, where she would undoubtedly place a headstone and flowers and grieve periodically, in an almost human way.

Now, in front of him, she began to cry, and he considered that he should, perhaps, hold her, console her for the pain he knew she felt. He could not bring himself to do so and instead passively watched her.

"It's not always so peaceful," the vet said, checking for a heartbeat. There was none. "I'll let you say your goodbyes," she added, leaving the room.

Jane gently stroked the cat's fur, then suddenly pulled back as the body was already stiffening and now gave the appearance of a stuffed toy rather than something that, moments before, had lived.

"We did the right thing," he told her. "He'd only have lived another week and been in pain. His liver was gone. You spared him some pain."

"But not myself," she blurted, turning away from the cat and shielding her face in her hands. "He was my cat. I had him before we were married. I feel like part of my life has died as well."

"He had a damned good life. He ate better than we did. He slept on the bed between us, and he peed wherever he felt like. He was a fat cat who got damned lucky."

"You don't understand," she said, walking out and leaving him alone with the corpse.

"But I do," he said to the cat. "She killed you with all that fatty food she fed you. But what did she do to me?"

In the car on the way home, she was silent, staring at the fields slipping by. Ahead a stray cat sat curbside, watching the car as it approached. She looked but paid it no attention.

"Do you think he felt any pain?" she finally said.

"No pain. He was purring right up until his heart stopped. Not a bad way to go, really."

"I miss him already," she said. "It won't be the same without him."

"Nothing will be the same," he said, knowing it to be the truth; the cat's illness merely brought to the surface the years of resentment following the incident. And selfishly, he found himself glad of the cat's death for the pain he knew it caused her.

"You just don't understand what I'm feeling."

"I understand more than I'm given credit for."

"He was my child, my baby. We never had any children, so he was *it*."

"Your choice, not mine."

"We didn't need children," she said.

"You didn't need children."

He pulled the car into the driveway and got out. He was standing in front of the house he always considered hers—she had picked it.

It was a small brick house surrounded by pine trees. She had decorated it, selected the shrubbery and the flowers and the cobblestones and, on the inside, the furniture and the color of the paint on the walls, in the same way that she had selected the pattern of their dishes and the design of the bed sheets, all of which, at this moment, he hated more than he knew he could ever express.

And he had allowed her those pleasures because it made her happy, and, at the time, he just wanted her to be happy, just as the fat cat sleeping between them made her happy.

It was not his house. It held none of his persona. And standing by the front door, he knew he would become the stranger he already felt he was.

Inside, she wandered through the rooms noticing the emptiness before settling on the couch. She told him so, and he shrugged and replied, "Only now?" and, with a nod, apologized for the cruelty of the statement.

"Why even apologize when you don't mean it?"

"Let's not start," he said, pouring himself a scotch and her a large glass of sherry, knowing she would be starting on something more volatile, such as the half-empty Southern Comfort she kept hidden in the garage behind the laundry supplies.

He handed her the glass and raised his in a toast. "To the cat," he said, "who was lucky enough to have an easy life and a quick way out." He took a large sip.

She sat silent for a moment and sipped at her drink before speaking. "I had hoped that things had changed with us," she said.

"Things never change."

"More's the pity. You can't just forgive me, can you?"

"Forgive? That's easy. Forgetting is the part I can't seem to do. Knowing that it was so incredibly stupid . . . ." He took another sip, and shook his head. "Rehashing again, I suppose . . . ."

"To hell with you," she hissed and finished her drink with a gulp.

"Do you remember the plant you got when we were first together?"

She nodded. "I bought it right after we made love the first time."

"And the antique, Oriental, glass paintings I used to own that you hated?"

"They broke. The frame wasn't strong enough to hold it."

"Not after you threw the salt shaker at it. And even though you said that the plant would grow with our love, it knew something you didn't. It died."

"And you're glad the cat died, even though you'd never admit it."

"I don't begrudge the cat. But you, you could have told him 'no,' that your marriage meant something more than getting drunk and giving in.'

"Damn you," she shouted, charging from the room and slamming the door behind her.

"No, damn you," he found himself screaming after her. He poured himself another drink. The cat got lucky, he thought.

In the next room, he could hear her crying. He wanted to pack his bags, walk out, and relish the revenge he wished so desperately he could obtain.

How could I ever trust you again, he thought? How could I leave you alone and not wonder? All his life, he had expected that he would have a marriage of trust and love, and in his mind, he knew that he could never have betrayed her in the way she had betrayed him.

It had felt as though his life had ended, like someone had sliced a section from him, a lump of flesh seething with all the lost hope and idealism.

Their wedding picture in a tarnished silver frame stared back at him. There were two happy people he could not remember. They looked happy, almost certain of the choice they had just made, moments before the flash went off. Like thoughts of the cat, those moments seemed muted now.

He went back outside and stared in through the window. It was quiet outside; the cool air pressed comfortably against him. Safety in silence, he considered.

He watched as she came from the bedroom, a wrinkled tissue in her hand, and sat down on the couch.

The motions felt right, he thought. He looked away, then back again.

He watched as she came from the bedroom and sat down on the couch next to the fat cat.

He would go inside in a moment and tell her he was leaving. He looked at the cat. The cat's liver was infected, and swollen, and he was on medication to flush out the toxins. The cat had a fifty-fifty chance. They would know tomorrow, although he felt the cat was already a goner.

The motions felt right. They felt comfortable, and well, they should, for he had practiced this scenario for a week.

What if the cat had to be put to sleep? He considered how cruel it would be to leave her on a Friday night and have to have the cat put to sleep on Saturday morning. And yet he knew he could not stay. Each day he remained was like living life as an endless pattern, forever renewing and becoming ever harder to change.

He watched her on the couch, petting the cat. *This is not my house*, he told himself, expecting the cameras to pull back and the final credits of this God-awful movie to roll up the screen. *This is not my life.*

He would walk in, and she would look at him. And she would see the expression of detachment in his eyes and know that what was to follow would hurt her, for she knew nothing other than the fact that she needed him in her life, even if she had hurt him repeatedly.

"I can't stay here," he would say, and she would frown and not make it easy for him.

"What do you mean you can't stay here? Don't be ridiculous. What are you talking about?"

'Us," he would mutter. "I can't live like this anymore."

And her eyes would glaze over, and the beginnings of a tear would form. "What are you telling me? Do you want a divorce?"

And his heart would skip a beat because hearing that word come forth from her mouth meant both pain and freedom, the former from the destruction of union, if even only in formality, and the latter from the relief of the burdens he had been carrying with him. "Divorce" was a word of power to be served up like a good cocktail.

"Yes," he would say. He had trained himself to say that word, not allowing the guilt or the thoughts of intense pain that he would be causing her to stop him this time; she had caused the same pain upon him to such a degree that he could no longer live with it. "I want a divorce," he would say slowly, clearly, savoring the fact that, finally, he would get the last word.

"Oh God!" he imagined that she would mutter, believing that a more accurate response would be a belligerent acceptance of the proposal.

In his pocket, he fingered the house keys, feeling the jagged edges, biding his time. He could feel the pressure of the outside coolness guiding him.

Perhaps the cat would live, he thought, sliding the key into the lock and turning the handle.

As the door opened, he could see the cat on the couch next to her. It looked up at him for the briefest of moments before closing its eyes, its head falling gracefully. Peacefully.

CHAPTER THREE
THE HOLLOW SKY

"Remember this, that very little is needed to make a happy life." ~ Marcus Aurelius

---

THERE WAS NO *SATORI*, which, for the Japanese, meant that there was no enlightenment.

From his cubicle, five up from the central walkway, Robert Yamato considered this fact. He had been a faithful employee since exiting school, trained by the corporation to suit their standards. This was the way it was in the world, the only expectation that a young boy could have; without the corporation, there was no chance for a decent life.

He was surrounded by walls, one-hundred levels in height, seven feet in depth, and endless in length; pock-marked with cubicles—what they called *Ansich*, a word derived from German that meant "in-itself" or "self-contained."

Ansich was made of dura-plastic, stronger than concrete, yet lightweight and modular. Each cubicle extended the length of the human body, with many compartments built around the surface for storage of all the necessities of the body living within. This included the sleeping mat—rolled up during the day—a small desk, a toilet seat that swung out from the side, and what few precious possessions the resident held; Robert Yamato only had a small wood carving of a sparrow. The wood had come from the disposal chute, having fallen to the floor unnoticed. He had whittled the sparrow over the last year and polished the wood with left-over oil from the meal tray that he had soaked in a small rag, and secreted away. He had never seen a sparrow but from paintings in the wall panels along the walkway below.

A bioluminescent panel above his head provided the lighting, and a thin roll-down cover sealed off the entrance hatch: the cliff edge that overlooked the central walkway offered the only view, varied depending on the level from which it was viewed.

This was the world of Japanshu, a self-contained city, and there was none other quite like it. Robert Yamato was Japanshu born and raised, as his parents and grandparents had been before him, none of whom he had met. Once school age, along with all the other children, he attended residential school: ten-hour school days and life within packed dormitories. Everyone worked. Even the children. That was the way. Work was the essence of value; he reminded himself.

Now, at age thirty-five, he was perched at the entrance hatch of his *Ansich*, work completed for the day, gazing out at the lines of the wall diminishing into the distance on all sides. There it was, he considered, perfection in architecture, certainly in accordance with the *Tao*; no beginning and no end.

The man in the next cubicle was likewise looking, glancing a cocked head toward Robert periodically as if to catch his attention. Robert did not know the man's name, only that, like a sparrow, he perched at the edge of his cubicle and cocked his head as if to study him.

"It is a lovely day," the man said after a bit. Robert nodded without looking back.

Beneath him, five levels down, a line of people was passing. From his vantage point, he was close enough to see their heads. Some were full-headed, others balding, some in patches. That line, too, stretched into a virtual infinity, a perpetual single-file of humanity on their way to the feeding area or simply out for exercise. There were no other reasons to leave *Ansich*. With a surplus of living beings, the need for social contact was limited strictly to the vid-screens in each cubicle. Even then, it was usually reserved strictly for business purposes.

Across from him and to the left and right, the facing walls of cubicles offered the same vantage point. He could see others peering out, coming and going like ants.

Here, there was no such thing as romance or dating. There was no sex unless mandated by the corporation as the need for workers increased. Any urges one felt were either contained silently, or released manually, not unlike other bodily functions with specially built devices—masturbation units—that served solely to relieve tensions, mute the drive for mating, or worse, dating.

He remembered a verse from Zen history:

The body is like unto the Bodhi-tree
The mind is like the stand of a bright
mirror
Carefully we cleanse it hour-by-hour
Lest dust should fall upon it.

He allowed himself a controlled breath, and felt his agitation calmed for a moment. He always found his thoughts disquieting; questions of value, purpose, and self-worth rising above the programming, above the conditioning that was always present. And of that, he dared not speak; such folly was a waste of energy. There was no why, only Japanshu, work, duty, honor, and nothing more. This should be enough for any man, he had been told upon his first day after schooling ended.

Beneath, he spotted a familiar face; his business associate from Tashami Electronics. She passed by without looking up, just one of many in that long line of bodies moving. Nonetheless, the swellings within him were quite powerful, and his eyes tracked her movement with possessive compassion.

You were in my dreams last night, Miss Tashami, he thought, as his eyes followed her steady shuffle into the distance. But it was a lie because he had barely managed to sleep at all; the steady shuffling of feet through the shift changes kept him awake, despite the slipcover sealing his entrance hatch. And it was a lie because such desires could not be acted upon, certainly not by choice. A terrible surge of loneliness washed over him, not for the first time in his life.

"World of walls," he said to himself, "you offer no compassion and no love. And yet, are we not made for love?" He glanced around the other cubicles and pondered how many others had enjoined the same thought.

In his right hand, he held three coins. He tossed them onto his sleeping mat and marked the first line of the hexagram. Then again, until the six lines of the hexagram were complete. *Ko*. He had looked it up in the *I Ching*, the historic record of all truths he might find. It was comforting that this had survived the changes of time. All cubicles held a copy with the accompanying coins.

Ko was the hexagram of changes. Line one denoted change at an early period. Line two signified brightness, and intelligence. That was hopeful. *Let the subject take action in the way of change.* Line three disposes the subject toward reckless and violent changing; this would be a bad omen unless caution was exercised. The next line vitiates any action, and requires the opportunity for repentance. But other conditions determine the opposite effect. Line five showed the Lord of the Hexagram. *The action will be beneficial.*

It was line six that truly caught his attention; he read it aloud: "The sixth, six, divided, shows the superior man as the leopard changes, while small men change their faces. To go ahead would lead to evil; but there be good fortune in abiding firm."

Robert considered this reading. He was unsure what a leopard was, having never seen one, and quickly tapped the definition on the keyboard. The vid-screen gave him the answer: Tiger-like. A member of the cat family. Spotted. Dangerous.

He shut the book and tossed it aside. Change had been on his mind for some time. He had inadvertently found his mind drifting, even during the work shift, questioning the purpose of his life. As intensive as programming code was, his mind would flit from thought to thought. He wanted more. But more than that, he wanted someone with whom to be close. He wanted sex. He wanted love. Both forbidden to the likes of him; someone on level five, far too low to be of value, far too low to create change.

He recalled a dream where a man and a woman would make love, and a baby would be born to them. They would raise the child. Robert Yamato could not imagine how that would work in *Ansich*, unless there were larger modules elsewhere in Japanshu. He had no idea. His world had extended to the Food Hall, the Bathing Hall, and then to the elevators that would take him to his work level. It was all quite straightforward. There were no maps to show you the way. You were told where to go on the first day of advancement, and you just remembered. You were one cog in the machine; all cogs were required to make the process advance smoothly, and no one wanted to be the one disrupting the flow.

Morning brought nourishment in the Food Hall, sixty paces down, in a direction to his left, and then a sharp turn right. It was a massive room filled with rows of tables and attached bench seats. Each person would line up and receive a tray, molded indents of a bowl and plate pre-formed, and it would be given, complete with food, beverage, medication, and utensils. They had set seating. No matter your position in the line, your seat remained waiting for you. Upon completing the allotted fifteen-minute meal allowance, the tray was dropped into a receptacle by the exit, and you would be back on the main track, continuing in the same direction for another four hundred paces to arrive back at your cubicle. There, an allotted ten minutes of hygiene would take place before reporting for work.

Pride dictated that you worked on a level that reflected your advancement and dedication to Tashami Electronics. He was now working on level 5, which offered hatch views of the desolate, urban interior landscape. Only above level 100 were there actual window views of the outside world. He often dreamed what it would be like, never having ventured outside.

Considering that when he first started to work, he was at sub-level 50, windowless and dark, processing ores that would end up as components in Tashami Electronic products, he had advanced quickly. If he lived long enough and continued his rate of advancement, he could expect to reach the 200th level within a decade. At that level, his accommodations would change; he would become a decision-maker, and he would have a larger cubicle. He had heard of the perks for the level 200 employees; better food, and special amenities such as soft massage sessions from sing-song girls. However, all was hearsay; no one had actually met anyone from that level. It was, however, a pleasing thought.

So it was only fitting that today's hexagram would match his thoughts of change. But change to what degree? Should he speak with Miss Tashami? There was no indication that she would listen; after all she was a stranger to him beyond the vid-screen. And then there was the matter of her affiliation with the corporation itself, her family name reflecting that association; she was one granddaughter of the company president. He had no way of knowing how that all worked short of asking, and that would be a rude affront he would never make.

Rolling up his sleeping mat, he placed it within the cabinet by the head. His desk was only half inserted into the wall cavity, papers strewn across the surface. The vid-screen flashed the day's agenda, which he had not yet begun to tackle.

There was no point in waiting for Miss Tashami's return since the central pathway extended only with one direction of motion. To return, one would have to follow the pathway behind his wall, which would eventually connect back to the central pathway. She would return to her cubicle unnoticed by him. And that was probably just as well. He had no idea where her cubicle was located. He realized that he did not, in fact, know very much at all.

For a time, he continued to watch the moving line of humanity, a steady, hypnotic flow in the same direction. He found his eye tracking one head until it was far off, then back to one that was just below. He had come to accept this as a way to calm himself, this separation from the self, the removal of his own identity, as he passively observed the motion of those he had no desire to meet. There was an order to this, and he was serene within the framework of the architecture, for he had known no other, although he could imagine another way.

"I wonder if others watch us," the voice of his neighbor interrupted. This time he turned to look at him. The man was not unlike himself. His head jutted out the opening so that he could see those below.

"Another time and place," Robert said. "Is it not a fountain within a stone garden that provides an inner tranquility?"

The man stared back and nodded sheepishly, having no idea to what Robert was referring.

Returning to his desk, he carefully stacked the papers into a neat pile. Here was where order stopped. His inability to sleep had hurt his ability to work. The business no longer mattered to him. And then, as if to further wound himself, he considered that he had never met his employers, never seen any of the products which his company made, or known the progress in any form other than sales figures. It was all sales figures that flashed across his vid-screen. There was no earned income, merely work credits, not that there was much to do with them. Everything was provided. To work for the corporation meant you were a physical part of the corporation, a necessary cog in a machine of a million cogs, together and yet not a collective.

He punched up the number for Tashami Electronics, then sat in front of the vid-screen waiting for his call to be answered.

Presently the face of a young woman filled the screen.

"Miss Tashami," he said softly. She closed her eyes and bowed slightly, enough for the movement to be well pronounced over a video connection.

"May I be of service, Mister Yamato?" she asked.

He smiled. "Please, I request that you call me Robert."

"May I be of service . . . Robert?" She blushed. At least it appeared that way on the screen.

"It is not business that I wish to discuss, Miss Tashami," he said. "I thought that I would merely inquire into your health, today?"

"I am well," she said, her eyes looking away for a moment, avoiding his. "If I may be so direct . . . Robert . . . it is an unusual question to ask from a business associate, is it not?"

Now he looked away, not sure for a moment, just how

to reply. "I beg forgiveness if I have cast insult to you, Miss Tashami," he finally said, studying her soft face for any indication of her thoughts. Her skin was pale, flawless. Her eyes, set like dark jewels, yet warm to look at. That was all he could see of her.

"No insult was taken, Robert," she said. "I was merely curious why you had asked. Forgive my boldness." She smiled at him.

"There is nothing to forgive," he told her, smiling back, feeling more confident now. "The fault was mine. I have been feeling quite distracted these past few days. I confess to admiring your inner beauty and your spiritual calm, Miss Tashami."

He looked directly at her and their eyes touched. Now, he told himself. I must know. "May I call you Alice? I feel we have been acquainted sufficiently for first names."

She paused for a moment, then smiled. "Please," she told him.

Robert Yamato inhaled deeply. "I am lonely, Alice."

The revelation changed him. His mind now flooded with images, foreign images. He thought of the two of them. Together. Change? Yet it was just the images, the strength of which was based on purity, sensations created not of the body; but from the mind.

The sin of weakness is the failure of the human heart, he told himself. Surely I have sinned. And yet the next words he had uttered after the revelation had been far worse: enough for Alice Tashami to quickly decline and sever their communication: He had asked her to visit him so that they might meet face to face for the first time.

Now he lay sprawled across his sleeping mat, ashamed and yet feeling better for having at least spoken his mind. It was a foolish thing to have done. And he was a fool for even having considered it. It was the book's fault for filling his head with ideas of change and chance. And yet how could there not be progress from change? How could an idea remain confined? To remain unchanged was to accept death. He did not wish to die. But now the flood-gates had been opened, impulsive, corrupting, and worse...unsubstantiated beyond the flood of emotions he felt. To have been so bold was risky to his future, and he knew there would be a price for this action. Every action has an equal and opposite reaction, he thought, reminding himself of the oracle Isaac Newton, who had first divined gravity's intentions.

From his mat he could see the cubicles on the adjacent wall and at least twenty with open hatches. He watched these other people fulfilling their destiny, oblivious to the perils of non-conformity. Where would it lead? he wondered.

And silently, he prayed for guidance. He heard a chime in the background. His monitor flashed a message. Turning to read it, he felt a wave of nausea sweep over him.

Robert Yamato

Level 5

Efficiency rating=0

Report to Hall of Greatness, Level 199

He sighed. This was not a good omen. Not good at all.

Calmly, he descended onto the central walkway from his ladder and followed it to the main elevator shafts at two-hundred paces. He summoned a module to take him up. The line continued past him, without him, unaware, and suddenly he felt alone and vulnerable.

When the module arrived, he entered and pressed for level 199. There were untold-hundred above-ground levels of Japanshu and he realized he had never passed level 5. There had been no reason. In fact, he had never been summoned upstairs before. As the module ascended and the lines of symmetry from the walls and people converged, he wondered whether he would be allowed to return.

Through the clear plastic, he could see each level as he passed. Each the same design, identical in every way except for the inhabitants. Passing the 100th level, the lower world gave way, a dividing ceiling/floor separating the two. He realized he could see no people now, empty hallways with pathway lights along the floors. Devoid of people, it felt cold and lifeless. At some point, he knew, people would fill those levels, promotions from within, as always, working your way up the ranks to the levels of more importance. Yet, he wondered why there were no people there now.

He could only dream of such a thing inasmuch as he could only dream about love. Love. Miss Tashami. Was that love? He knew so little of such things; inexperienced and kept that way. Japanshu was control, and loyalty was obedience.

There was no *Tao*.

The module stopped, and its doors opened. Ahead he saw a massive doorway and a hallway. There were no walls here and nothing to see. The answer was behind the door.

"Enter," a voice boomed out. It surrounded him and filled him with fear.

Cautiously he pushed open the doors and was struck by the vastness that stretched to an apparent infinity.

White, barren. He could hear his heart beating feverishly. He stood for a moment and bowed.

"Come forward," the same voice commanded. Silently he obeyed, his pace the same as it would have been on the main level, amidst the flow of human bodies all moving as one.

Minutes passed, or perhaps longer, he considered. It was cold and the chill sliced through him. White. Purity. I have found Shinto–the way of the gods.

"More," the voice instructed. "Closer."

He looked back and could no longer see the great doors. Even the ceiling and walls blended into a white haze. A spasm shook his lower jaw, and he clenched his teeth to silence the chattering.

Stopping for a moment, he buried his face into his hands, avoiding a wash of nausea and dizziness. "What have I done?" he muttered.

"Continue," the voice told him, and he stumbled to his feet and lunged forward faster, barely able to control his movements until he was running, or more appropriately, falling forward, feeling the pull of an invisible gravity; falling but never hitting the floor, like the dreams of his shattered sleep.

And then, before him appeared a kneeling pad, small, distinct—all that was visible. *It rushes to me*, he told himself, *or I to it*.

With a sigh, he fell onto it, panting uncontrollably. He

wiped his eyes to clear the haze and felt wetness. And he waited for what was to come next.

For minutes there was only silence.

"Our ancestors lived in honor," the voice said calmly. "Our ancestors did not live in shame."

Robert nodded in a short bow.

"You have dishonored yourself, Yamato-san. You are aware of what I speak?"

"I have dishonored myself," Robert repeated.

"The pride in work and in spirit of us all has been dishonored," the voice told him. "You have chosen to discard our values and our honor. Now there can only be disgrace and dishonor."

"Please," he shouted, then lowered his voice. "The shame and dishonor is mine to bear. It was not my intention to bring shame to Japanshu or to my employer. I must clear the shame."

"Honor and obedience. The way of truth. These are the values of a well-lived life. The one is the sum of the totality."

And Robert Yamato heard himself say,"All I can do I will. Happily, I will forfeit my life. I will forfeit and repair the honor for honor's sake."

Beside him a *wakizashi*, a short sword, appeared. Nine and a half inches in length, it reached to a point with an edge that he knew to be razor-sharp. It was an instrument of surgical precision. A tool for a rapid death.

He studied it, aware that this small thing would end, for him, the incessant conflict that had consumed him for so long. Strangely he did not fear it; he almost welcomed the prospect of eternal peace.

Slowly he reached for it and brought it to him, raising it reverently to eye level with both hands before placing it before him again. The wooden handle was wrapped in cloth, and tightly wound to facilitate a solid grip.

"I alone accept the dishonor I have caused," he said. "For this I remove the shame of Japanshu, and I beg of you, who are here with me, to do me the honor of bearing witness to my act."

"All Japanshu will witness restoration of honor," the voice said.

Robert had not known that this would be broadcast throughout the city. Alice would be seeing his death. I will perish thinking of her, he thought. The pain will be brief and I will find freedom. I will have found *satori*.

He opened his shirt, exposing smooth bare skin, then picked up the blade and turned it to lightly touch his exposed stomach. He gripped the handle with both hands firmly, overlaying the fingers of one hand over the top of the other hand for a better grip. He looked blankly ahead, clearing his mind of fear. It would be painful, he knew, but it would be swift. He inhaled deeply to calm his mind.

Miss Tashami, he thought, *Alice*, seeing her face in his memory one last time, then, with one sudden jolt, he snapped the blade toward him to welcome the abyss he knew would engulf him.

In the instant of searing pain, which his mind had warned him would come first, he felt only his hand brushing against his belly as he twisted the blade hard to both sides and then, with another hard twist, straight up before withdrawing it from his body. It will be over in a moment, he thought.

He heard the blade hit the floor, and his eyes looked at it with surprise. There was no blood on it. He glanced down to his wound and touched it with both hands. Again no blood on his hands. He looked down at his bare skin. No wound. Nothing. His mind reeled. He looked again at the blade where it had fallen, but it was now gone.

"Honor is restored," the voice said calmly. "The total harmony of the world has been reborn, and the sins have been removed. Return to life, Yamato-san, and bear witness to a life without sin."

Robert Yamato sat dazed for a moment. Then he stood slowly, bowed, barely able to control the trembling in his limbs or the rushing of blood to his brain. He gingerly took a step, lost his balance, and fell. Then he stood again, turning back from where he had come.

The tears flowed easily now, no longer in shame or fear; rather from the rebirth he had just experienced.

"Follow me," the voice, now soothing, told him. "I will

tell you the Tale of Harmony as you walk." Robert nodded.

"The humble ant has crossed the path where many tread, unaware of the danger of its passage. Like you, it must understand the possibility that life may be fleeting, yet still it proceeds. No caution can be taken since the speed at which the ant travels is slow compared to those of the people passing. Still, the ant continues, immovable to its destiny."

The great door was just ahead.

"In this way you are the ant, passing through the unknown. Around you is *Tau*. Within you is choice. This is the mystery of life which you have now received. Carry its truth with you. In peace."

At the end of the hallway, he stopped to take in the view from the window before returning to his level. Before him was a landscape devoid of color; a reddish-brown hue uniformly spread out. He could see other corporate towers, different worlds beyond his reach, each unto itself, a whole. There was no greenery between them, certainly not like within the Zen gardens of Japan-shu. Aerocars travelled across the sky in single file lines, and Robert wondered where they were going, small specks of irrelevancy untold in the annals of his world. Staring out only amplified the emptiness he felt. There was no joy to be found there.

The great doors opened before him, and he stepped

into the waiting module. The levels slipped passed, no longer his concern, and, in the next instant, he was again beneath the ceiling of the first hundred levels and then onto the central pathway.

There was work to be done, he reminded himself, his mind still reeling from the experience.

As he stepped from the ladder into his cubicle, he had already planned the rest of the day divided into a series of tasks. First, he would straighten the mess. He removed his shirt and put it aside, then withdrew a fresh shirt from one of the cabinets and put it on.

The vid-screen flashed his messages. Miss Tashami had called. *Twice.* He stared at the screen for a moment, buttoning his shirt, and then hesitantly pressed for a return call. Her face quickly filled the screen.

"I am returning your call, Miss Tashami. I apologize for my absence," he said calmly.

She stared at him, silent for a few seconds. "You do not look well, Robert," she said. "Are you in good health?"

He shook his head. "No. May I assist you in some matter?"

She looked away, uncertain if she should continue. "I regret my previous reaction. Your request caught me by surprise, and I reacted badly. I have thought of what you have asked and even though it is illogical, I find that it remains in my mind. If you are still willing, I would very much like to see you."

Robert stared at her face, that face that had been so ingrained into his mind. He remembered his time upstairs. His mind replayed the blade slicing into him. It had been a warning, one not to be taken lightly.

"I am afraid that is not possible," he told her. "I have much work to do. I have been . . . deficient. But now I have been restored. Honor has been restored."

He watched her face for a reaction and could see that she knew exactly what had happened; the audio had been played throughout Japanshu, the visuals projected onto the large screens in the halls for all to see. Of course, no one would speak of it to him. It would remain unmentionable. No one would ask questions. There was nothing to say. Everyone understood the message as well as Robert did. And yet . . . Alice had still messaged him. *Why?*

"Forgive me," she said quickly. "I have made an error of judgement. Apologies." She bowed, and the connection was broken.

Childish whims, he thought to himself, yet he could still see her face from a previous call when she had smiled at him. He had enjoyed, very much, making her smile. Her smiles warmed him in many ways, both physically and emotionally. She brought a calm over him, a sense of purpose beyond the work he was required to do.

Ko was the hexagram of changes. He remembered that it was line six that truly caught his attention. He recited it from memory: "The sixth, six, divided, shows the superior man as the leopard changes, while small men change their faces. To go ahead would lead to evil; but there be good fortune in abiding firm."

He considered what the voice had told him; he was just the ant oblivious to the path of the larger world, the ant passing through the unknown.

"There is no room for this," he told himself. "It defies the way." Again, images of her face formed in his mind. Her smile. How she looked at him. He knew that it meant something, even if he was uncertain the extent. He knew that she filled that part of him that was as barren as the view he had witnessed above.

And then, again, he remembered that he had almost died upstairs, had committed himself to restoring lost honor which he falsely believed was due to his interest in her. But he had not died; the blade had been an illusion, so what had he truly lost?

And even as the blade had sliced into him, it was *her* face that he had held onto, the last image he wished to see–the last feeling he wished to experience. Surely that held far greater meaning than the Tale of Harmony, spoken to him by an unseeing face, who had offered him an imaginary blade. The leopard changed, he thought to himself, no longer fearful.

"You're back," his neighbor said to him, leaning out so as to be able to peer into Robert's cubicle.

"Yes," Robert replied flatly.

"Are you well?"

"I am well . . . enough," he replied. Then . . . "What is your name?"

The neighbor smiled. "I am Arakan," he said. "And you are Robert."

"I am Robert. I thank you for your ongoing politeness," he told the man. "It is kind of you."

"And to you," Arakan said, ducking back into his cubicle, pleased with himself.

A message flashed red across the vid-console accompanied by a chime. It read: *Robert Yamato, programmer, class 2, transfer request approved to level 50, unit 525. Please proceed to relocate immediately.*

How odd, he thought. I did not request any transfer. That he would now be on level 50 did not displease him. He peered out of his cubicle and looked up. There were 100 levels to this section, and then countless-hundreds beyond the ceiling above.

He wondered whether his discipline had triggered the transfer, a way to pacify him while still retaining control. And how long before the new status would become as the old one, just a different vantage point. Above level 100 no one knew of others, no association, communication, mingling. Their world was quite different—apart. *Perhaps they all have windows above that level,* he thought, although having seen the view through the window himself, he knew it was unaffecting. He had not, however, seen any people as he traveled up. Were there no people there?

And then he wondered why they did not let him die; why the illusion of death was enough. Was it just to restrict him from further feelings? He was but one of the millions. One ant. Who would notice his death? Or was he really one of millions?

He summarized the experience in his mind. He had been rewarded for indulging in the forbidden. Had Alice likewise been corrected? Probably not, given her status as an important granddaughter.

A wave of thoughts cascaded upon each other. He should not have ended their last communication. That she had contacted him to agree to meet told him that he was not alone in how he felt. He wondered how many others felt as they did?

He reached for the figurine of the sparrow he had made, ran his fingers across the well-worn surface. This was his sole, non-utilitarian possession, and he treasured it. Only now, he wished to gift it to Alice. Without the joy it would give to her, it held little meaning for him beyond an indulgence. It was all about her, every conceived moment of pleasure and joy.

Were he to proceed, would he be sentenced to death?

Would they both be excised from Japanshu, left to wander the desolate world beyond without belonging to any society, without protection? And yet, to remain, sterile in thought and deed, was no option either. He had seen the sky and felt its hollow song. And then there was her face, fresh in his mind, as always, her skin so pale and soft like a flower petal, her eyes so intense when she stared at him. And her smile . . . . He stared at the sparrow in his hand and stroked its head once again. He was smiling.

Quickly, he dialed her number.

"Please, Alice," he said the moment her face appeared. "Come now."

CHAPTER FOUR
JUST A LITTLE DEATH

"Life is what happens to you while you're busy making other plans...." ~John Lennon (from the song 'Beautiful Boy.')

I HAD BEEN THERE before during the days of my youth and I remembered them now as vividly as when I had been there. As I turned off the main road and down the final stretch, which led to the main gates, the years returned; I had never really left.

I had been there when the roads were thick with gravel, such as new roads are inclined to be, when we would all walk to breakfast, from the house at one end to the dining hall at the other; we were freshly showered, wearing the uniforms which, over the years, had faded slightly, no longer crisp, nor fresh-smelling. Although I had been there for so long, then, in so many moods, it was to that time that my heart returned as I approached.

The air was crisp—it had always been crisp, even in the heat of summer—and the scent of pine and freshly mowed grass saturated it. Ahead, the clock tower loomed over me as I passed through the wrought-iron gates and came to a stop at the headmaster's house. The house was set within a small, floral garden that seemed to excrete color—no doubt the handiwork of the headmaster's wife—and in front, two large cricket ovals, still well-tended, even after all the years, spread past the crescent of red-brick houses—the dormitories.

The headmaster emerged from the house before I had stepped out of my car, a stocky man of fifty-five, smartly dressed in slacks and a tweed jacket. He trotted toward me with a slight wave.

"David. Welcome."

I stepped out and was overwhelmed by a momentary uncertainty about my return; had I become a student once again?

"Mr. Fisher," I said, extending my hand and shaking his.

“Douglas, please," he chided, pleasantly.

"Of course. Sorry. It's a difficult habit to break."

"You'll get used to it. Come, you must be tired from your trip. Ann's making some tea. We can settle you in later. There's no rush. Most of the students won't get here till late this afternoon."

"Fine. Thank you."

We walked up the small stone pathway and into the house. I had been inside only once before, on my first day as a student. The hallway was lined with gold-framed portraits of previous headmasters, and I scanned them for any familiar face.

"I don't think you'd know any of them," the headmaster said. "I know I don't, but then most of these are the early ones. The others are in the dining hall. You were here during Robert Garnish's time, weren't you?"

"Yes. That's right."

"Yes, of course. Nice man. Met him once, just before he passed away. About six years ago now. We had a memorial service for him in the chapel."

"That's too bad."

"Yes, quite," he said, leading me further into the house,"but then we all have to go some time. Which house were you in? Perry?"

"No. Barrymore. I almost went to Scott-Francis."

"Barrymore's a good choice. It's fitting, then, that you'll be taking it over. Ah, Ann, David's just arrived."

The headmaster's wife joined us. She was a foot

shorter than her husband, and her hair was curled slightly, an auburn tint which I guessed made the grey less obvious. She smiled, as though we had previously met, and held out her hand for me.

"David, Welcome."

"Thank you, Mrs. Fisher. It's nice to see the place again."

"Would you care for some tea? I've just put some on."

"That would be nice."

"I was just telling David how fitting it is that he'll be getting Barrymore. It was his old house."

"Oh good. That's wonderful. You must be eager to get settled."

"A little. I get the feeling, though, that I'm still a student. It will feel strange moving into the master's house."

The headmaster's wife smiled. "You'll get used to it. When were you here?"

"Twelve years ago."

"I'm not sure if there's anyone left from then. We've had a lot of new teachers."

"I believe Smithers, from chemistry, was here then. Do you know him?" the headmaster asked.

The very mention of Smithers caused me to smile. "We used to call him the mad professor. He would start each chemistry class with an explosion just to get our attention. I remember, once, it set off the fire alarm and the sprinklers turned on. Poor Smithers was never the same after that."

The headmaster delighted in the story, emitting a silent laugh. His wife smiled politely, then excused herself to prepare the tea. When she had gone we sat down and the headmaster lit his pipe as I watched from across the coffee table. Through the stained-glass windows, through the ivy which had crept across the entire front of the house, I could see the lagoon. Years earlier I had rowed there, spending countless hours on weekends within the shaky confines of a single-man skull, sailing wherever the mild currents decreed and struggling to balance as I pulled in the oars. It was a tricky art. Alone out there, I could see the school as a panorama. It looked like an oil painting on display. Surreal.

Presently, after two cups of tea, and further conversation about my earlier days, I left and headed out across the two emerald ovals toward Barrymore, nestled comfortably on one end of the crescent, between a row of birch trees. I had run the circumference of the ovals every day for three years, goaded into running faster by old Weller, the instructor who, despite the fact that my stomach had knotted and that breakfast threatened a reprise, would shout, from across the field,"Train without pain, train in vain." And with the others on the team, I would run faster only to suffer the consequences much later, after a hasty dinner.

By night though, I would stroll the same stretch of grass, smothered by darkness and invisible to the houses around, watching everything, only the slight glow of the street lamps against the red-brick fronts, and finding a sense of security at being the only one awake.

Barrymore lay before me. My own housemaster had walked the corridors—which always smelled of ammonia from the deep cleaning—his heels smacking down on the hardwood floors. These were corridors which sunlight would splinter into; the light could never enter directly as it would diffract from the overhead stained-glass panels. The light would be streaks of red and navy blue and yellow; rarely would it be white. The housemaster would walk hard and firm, and from the study rooms, we would hear him approach, certain of who it was by the pace of his walk. We pretended to dislike him, convincing ourselves that he was a cold, hard man, and like all the other teachers, a pious, self-centered bastard. Would I become such to my students, I wondered?

The house was unlocked and I walked in. Before even checking my own section of it—the place where I would actually live—I began down the main corridor. The walls were dark stained wood and from them, hanging in rows were the plank boards with the names of each year's students carefully painted on them. I was listed in 1969, my name close to the bottom with three small stars beside it. They were the distinctions won: most of the students had won distinctions at some time.

There was a library at the end of the corridor which housed a modest collection of books, and next to that the assembly room which, for the rest of the time doubled as a television room. Supper would be offered at night, a cup of hot chocolate, and a few biscuits as a treat between study sessions.

The room was still the same. They had acquired a couch during my absence and it was the only thing that stood out.

"Hello, sir," a voice called from behind. I turned to face a boy of fourteen. He was wearing the blue school shirt, untucked, the grey slacks, and the house colors on his sweater—brown with a yellow stripe at the bottom.

"Are you the new housemaster?"

I nodded. "What's your name?"

"Jennings, sir. William Jennings, but you can call me Bill."

"Hello Bill. I am Mr. Wilson. I believe you're early?"

"Yes sir, but my father had to go to a meeting so he brought me in this morning. It is alright, isn't it?"

"Yes."

"Would you like me to show you around?" he offered eagerly.

"That's quite alright. I know my way. Oh, and tuck in your shirt. It's too early in the term to look scruffy."

"Yes sir." Hastily he complied.

"What form are you in?"

"Fifth, sir."

"I see. Well, I'm sure that you'll have a nice term. It's always been a good house."

"Were you a student here?"

"Yes."

"Then your name'll be on the boards."

"It is."

"That's great."

"Yes. Yes, I suppose it is. What sports will you be taking?"

"Football in the summer and cross-country in the winter."

"Soccer?"

"No, sir. Australian rules. My father says I'm pretty good at it."

"Well, then," I told him firmly, I'll expect a lot from you."

"Yes, sir."

He turned to walk away then turned back and smiled for a moment before walking out. A moment later I walked out only to find him standing beneath the boards, scanning the names.

"1969?" he called out.

"It would have been easier to ask," I replied. "Do they still have the old house photos on the wall somewhere?"

He pointed to the door at the other end of the corridor. "In the piano room."

I began to walk toward it, a steady pace so as to reduce the noise of my heels on the wooden surface. He followed. Inside, he leaped ahead of me, quickly finding the correct year and pointing to it. I shuffled forward for a closer look. The photograph had been taken toward the end of the year. We were in our Sunday suits, arranged in order of height, and, at the front, our housemaster sat, hands clenched and placed atop his knees. I was at the back, hair combed neatly to one side, looking no older than Jennings.

"Don't say it," I warned him, anticipating a reaction.

"I wasn't going to say anything," he protested. Then he asked,"Do you see any of them now?"

"A few." I pointed at one. "Solomon, there, died when he was hit by a car. A week after this picture was taken. And Thompson, there, died of a drug overdose last year. Binden now runs his father's company. They've all gone somewhere, grown up. One day you might come and take a look and wonder where they all went."

Jennings said nothing; he simply continued to stare as though the photograph held for him the same memories it held for me.

"Have you finished unpacking?" I finally asked.

"No, sir."

"Well off with you then. I'll have a bed check at ten and you'd better be unpacked by then."

"Yes, sir." He turned and raced for the door. I watched him leave, noticed the almost clumsy, yet almost controlled motions, and wondered whether I had moved like that.

I turned back to the photograph. Solomon had been my best friend. He had guided me through my early years there, always with a kind word at each of my disappointments, telling me how something good was almost sure to happen next. And he died before my eyes, one Sunday, during a trip into town. A car had swerved and struck him. I could still hear the thud of metal and flesh meeting violently, could see him thrown up over the hood and back onto the road as the car braked. But it was already too late; his neck had been broken in the impact.

I left the room of photographs and found my part of the house. I had been given several rooms. The living room was spacious. The school supplied some furniture, enough to flesh out the emptiness, but I would have to add to it.

I had brought five boxes with me. They were now in the living room. Most contained clothes and books, the few essential things until I could get home to bring the rest.

At seven-thirty in the evening, the assembly bell tolled, and I stood aside as a stream of bodies came thundering down the stairs. Then I entered and the room fell silent. The boys had clustered themselves in the center of the room, not at all how assemblies had been in my day there. All eyes upon me.

"Good evening."

"Good evening, sir," they chanted.

"Next time I would like you to assemble around the edge of the room in alphabetical order. That'll make roll call a lot easier. For those of you who have not met me, I am Mr. Wilson, your housemaster. I shall also be teaching in some of the English sets. And for those of you who might, at some time, whether it be now, or in the future, think me to be unrealistic, or overly hard, I take great delight in telling you that I was, once a student in this very house. I do remember how it feels. So I hope that any problems you might have you'll bring to my attention. I am a good listener.

"We'll be having an assembly every evening at seven-thirty, except on Fridays and Saturdays. Those of you who wish to go home on the weekends, or wish to leave the school grounds, must see me for a pass. Now, if there are no questions, you can go finish unpacking. I believe Matron will have supper for you shortly, and lights-out will be at ten-thirty. All right. That's all."

The congregation filed out as quickly as they had

arrived. I watched, felt the tug of youth nudge me briefly in the same direction as though, without warning, I might have started to run, feeling the tug of the school shirt as it worked its way out of my slacks. The urge, perhaps primordial, allowed me to find my old bed, buried within a row of beds within a dorm room which looked more like a hospital ward than a boarding room. But I remained fast, now alone in the large assembly room. The urge passed.

During supper, as the boys who were late stood in line for a cup of hot chocolate, I stood outside. The corridor was empty, yet held a fine mist which remained present in every section of the house, and outside, along the length of the ovals, and by the lagoon as it always had. The house had its own smell, aside from the ammonia-washed floors, and this seemed to spread much as the light, which had earlier, splintered in; traces felt in passing.

I walked back inside the assembly room.

"Sir," Jennings called out,"will you tell us something about when you were here."

"What do you want to know?"

"Did they have girls here then?" another boy asked.

"What's your name, first?"

"Anthony Bryant, sir."

"Yes, they had girls then, Bryant. That was the first year."

"Did you have a girlfriend, sir?" another asked. "I'm Peter Dynesdale."

"Yes, I did. Her name was Melissa."

"What became of her, sir?" Jennings asked.

"She's married. She married a friend of mine."

"Did you ever take her to the sheds?" somebody shouted from behind, disappearing from the room before I could turn around. The room came alive with laughter. I cast a questioning look at Jennings.

"That's Mitchell," he said. No sooner had he said it that he got angry glances from the others.

"You shouldn't squeal on your friends," I told him. He looked down. "And in answer to Mitchell's question, we didn't have the sheds then." The laughter returned.

"There's a girl in Jennings House, Cheryl Darling, and we call her honey," Bryant said. "You should go up to her and say can I call you honey, darling."

The boys all broke into laughter.

"I don't want to hear any name calling around here," I said.

The supper ended and the boys filtered out, careful to bypass Matron so as to avoid having to help her carry the urn of hot chocolate back to her quarters.

"Jennings," I said, just as he turned to leave, and motioned to Matron. With a frown, he complied, and I watched as he approached her, could hear the immortal words which, at one time or another, we had all uttered: "Matron, can I help you with something?" Matron smiled, a grandmother's smile of delight at her grandchild's thoughtfulness, before handing him the bulky urn. With a disapproving glance at me, Jennings struggled out of the room, Matron close behind with the tray of dirty cups.

I wandered through the corridors until ten-thirty, then rang the bell to signal lights-out before walking upstairs to the rooms. As I entered, two boys, still wet from their showers, pushed past me and quickly climbed into their beds. I made sure each bed was occupied, feeling the trace of the past sweeping over me—the splinter of old fear that I should quickly get into bed before the housemaster could notice that I was missing.

"Everything okay?" I said, then, "Goodnight." I flicked off the light switch, closed the door and waited.

"Jesus," someone inside shouted.

"Talk about strange."

"Crap," another joined in. "He's probably just matriculated."

"Balls," someone screeched

"He was here in sixty-nine," Jennings' unmistakeable voice hollered.

"Who gives a shit, Jennings, now shut up before I rearrange your ugly face."

"Oooh," someone else sneered. The voices diminished into hushed whisperings.

I walked down to the next room, the room in which I had slept as a student. My bed had now been overrun by a large boy who, as I glanced in somewhat nostalgically, returned my stare with an indignant expression.

"Any problems?" I asked. There was no reply. "Okay, goodnight then." I turned off the lights.

"Sir," a voice whispered through the dark. "I didn't mean to be rude, earlier."

"You're safe this time, Mitchell."

I walked out and closed the door, waiting for some counter-comment.

"I didn't mean to be rude, sir," someone mimicked in an effeminate voice. "I'm just a stupid little bugger."

The others began to laugh.

Later, having returned to my rooms, I sat down and contemplated my own unpacking. The rooms seemed empty, not that I had thought otherwise during the brief visits at the housemaster's requests, but more so now I was in charge. It was to be me who would make the decisions and govern the horde of teenagers. Somehow the room lacked authority.

As I slept, that night, images of rough, starched sheets scraping against bare legs returned to me. The beds of the dormitory were like rocks of protection, padded by the starched sheets and the starched pillows which somehow one would get accustomed to and later miss during the mid-term breaks. They fortified the character in some mysterious way, matching only the cold, wooden floors which, by morning, felt good to the touch. And despite the fourteen beds, and the large, authoritative dressers and closets, one could stand naked and feel a sense of space, of cool air circulating beneath arms and between legs after a hot shower—it was sensuous. Soft feelings for a hard place.

The images were more to do with sounds and smells than any one visual image, as if such a thing in a dream could actually be classified as an image of sorts, and each pervaded the mind, becoming more than just a scent, or a noise, but an integral part of the feeling of security, of being home.

It was to one such noise that I awoke; the telephone in the living room was ringing and had somehow become part of my dream. Hastily I got up, staggered toward it and answered its call.

"David. It's Charles."

"Charles?" I muttered.

"Listen, I've just received a call from Telly Longston, the aunt of one of your boys, Jennings, I believe. His parents were killed in a plane crash last night."

"Oh, no. That's terrible." The words echoed in my mind. Was this all a part of my dream? I wondered. "Should I tell him now, or wait until after he's awake? I suppose I should let him sleep. Yes, that would be best."

"David, tell him after the wake up bell. Then bring him over here. You come too. I'm sorry that this had to happen to you so early . . . for him too, of course. Can you manage on your own?"

"Uh, Yes, yes I'll be fine. There's no doubt, is there? I mean, they're absolutely sure?"

"His aunt identified the bodies an hour ago. It's tragic. See what you can do for him. You might want to let the other boys know, tell them to lay off him for awhile."

"Yes, of course. What time is it now?"

"Six-thirty. Not long to wait."

"Yes. Thank you for calling. I'll see what I can do and I'll bring him over."

"Fine, I'll see you then, David."

The line went dead. For a moment I held the receiver, as though, by some afterthought, he might have to add something. Then slowly, I placed it back.

A coldness crept over me. The room in which I was standing now seemed empty. And soon, I knew, I would be telling a boy of fourteen that both his parents had been killed. Yet I knew the words already for they returned from some dark abyss within that I knew too well.

I got dressed quickly, paced the room for fifteen minutes wondering when would be the right moment. With each moment the decision was for the moment following. And then for the next. But it could no longer wait: I had to let it out, had to release it before it could overwhelm; I had to be the rock, not the water.

I left my rooms, strode briskly up the stairs and along

the corridor to the room at the end, my heels smacking the floor. I opened the door and walked over to Jennings' bed. And there I stopped, staring down at a small boy curled vulnerably beneath the covers.

I shook him once, hard. His eyes opened, looked up at me.

"Get dressed and come down to my rooms," I said, flatly, then turned and strode out.

After a few minutes he appeared at my door, clad only in a robe and still half-asleep. I beckoned him in, motioned for him to sit as I closed the door, then, losing the harshness which I earlier projected, sat down next to him.

"I'm sorry for what I have to tell you," I began, noticing, already, the widening of his eyes,"but your mother and father died last night."

He said nothing, offered no trace of emotion beyond the slight widening of his eyes. Then he looked down. "How... did they die?"

"They were flying home. The plane . . . it crashed." My hand touched his shoulder, squeezed it and remained there. "I am so sorry."

"Dead," he muttered.

I nodded. "Don't worry about your classes. I'll square it away. After assembly we'll go to the headmaster's."

"It's not fair," he whispered. "It's just not fair, sir." Tears were brimming. I had to look away.

"I know it isn't, William. Will you be all right? Is there anything I can get you right now?"

"No."

"Listen, stay here while I take assembly. Will you be all right on your own?" He nodded.

"Good boy. I won't be long."

Outside the assembly bell was ringing. I closed the door behind me and walked to the assembly room. Inside, the boys had already lined up. I walked in and they stopped talking.

"Good morning," I began. "This will be short, no roll call. Most of you don't know that during the night, William Jennings' parents were killed in a plane crash . . . ."

"Shit," someone said from the far end of the room.

". . . I would appreciate it if you could desist from any derogatory comments, he's going to be going through a very difficult time. So be nice, or for those of you who can't manage that, lay off him for awhile. You don't want to cross me on this. Understand?" There were nods all around. "Okay, get ready for breakfast. That's all."

I turned and walked out, back down the hall to my rooms. Jennings was still seated, his head still down.

"Does my aunt know?" he asked.

"She telephoned the headmaster this morning. Would you like to call her? You can use the phone in here."

"No, maybe later."

"Whenever you're ready."

There was a knock on the door and it opened. One of the boys stood there, a school uniform folded, in his hands. He glanced nervously at me, then at Jennings.

"I thought you might need these," he said, offering the clothes to me. I took them, placed them down on the chair.

"I'm sorry, Bill," the boy said.

"Thanks, Tony."

"If you want to talk about it....Well, I'd better go," he said, turning and closing the door behind him.

"Why don't you get changed," I told Jennings,"and let's go to the headmaster's house."

Jennings stood, took off his robe, dropping it on the couch, and slipped on his pants and shirt. "Do I look okay?"

"No, but it doesn't matter," I said with a forced smile.

He nodded.

"William," Mrs. Fisher said,"I'm so terribly sorry." She leaned forward and pulled him toward her, held him awkwardly. Jennings offered no resistance, pulling back only when her grip had lightened.

"Come, please, let's sit down, have something to eat. It'll make you feel better," the headmaster said, motioning us into the dining room. The dining table had been set, laced table mats protected the table from the cutlery, and a small vase of roses filled the center space.

The headmaster pulled back a chair for Jennings, waved me to one on the other side and then sat down beside his wife. A pot of tea had been placed on the side-board and Mrs. Fisher reached for it and began pouring.

"William," the headmaster began,"have you spoken to your aunt yet?"

"No, sir."

"Well, I suggest after breakfast you give her a call. I'm sure she's worried about you."

"Yes, sir. I suppose." He looked away for a moment, then back at the headmaster. "Will I be able to stay here, I mean, now that . . . ?"

"Of course, of course you will," the headmaster hurriedly assured him. "Don't think about it now. We'll deal with that when the time comes, all right?"

"We can work something out," I added. I knew that it could be done.

"How about some bacon and eggs?" Mrs. Fisher suggested with a smile.

"No, thank you. I'm really not hungry."

"Oh, but you must eat something. Have just a little?"

"I couldn't."

"Don't force the boy, Ann," the headmaster told her. "He'll eat when he's ready."

"I told him that he's excused from classes," I added, quietly, almost out of a wish to avoid the silence which I knew to be approaching.

"Quite," the headmaster said. "There's no rush. He can go back when he feels ready for it. I'm sure his teachers will understand. I'll update them later."

Jennings looked up. "Would it be all right, sir, if I went for a walk? It'd make me feel better."

"Of course you can," Mrs. Fisher happily announced. The wear and tear of the conversation had already taken its toll on her ability to smile. The headmaster nodded his approval and Jennings stood and walked out. At the door he stopped and turned back to me.

"I'll be okay," he said.

After he had gone the headmaster let out a sigh. His brow was knitted, a deep frown distorting his features into an expression of anger.

"Damn," he hissed,"it's grossly unfair for something like this to happen to a child. Grossly unfair."

"Poor boy," Mrs. Fisher whined, the air of composure normally surrounding her now gone--she looked suddenly older, exhausted.

"David," the headmaster said solemnly,"stay with him today. No matter how much he may want to be alone, it always helps to have someone there,"

"Of course," I replied, noticing, in my voice, the slight

trace of indigence at the suggestion that I might not have thought to do so already. "He'll be okay," I quickly added.

"Would you like something to eat?" Mrs. Fisher asked.

"Thank you, no. Perhaps I'd better go after him, see where he goes?"

I stood. The headmaster gave an approving nod. I smiled at Mrs. Fisher, then left. I could understand why Jennings had wanted to be alone; the overwhelming sympathy within the headmasters house was too much even for those who had not experienced a loss.

As I walked back to Barrymore, the students were already on their way to classes, walking in the groups they had made, with friends who, quite like each other, relied on the same basic qualities to maintain a circle of friends. I could almost name them on sight; the groups of rebellious pranksters—these looked more tardy than the rest, milling closely together, laughing intermittently at some obscure remark made by one of the others, the group of true students, the intellectuals, immaculate in their uniforms, maintaining the same stride, the same pace and direction like a formation of fighter planes executing an aerial show, and the groups of those, who, for some reason or another, wound up together. These I referred to as the lost and founds. Their bond was weak—they might be in a class together, or on the music team, or on the debating society.

I had not belonged to any group; I was the one who

stood aside and watched with unbridled curiosity at the events and the relationships taking place around me. And I would listen from a distance to the conversations of the others, each, in turn, detailing their morbid sexual experiences with the school's girls, daring others to get them to the lagoon where most of the school's informal sexual education took place. By night, back then, walking the circumference of the ovals, one would have to tread warily so as not to step on the paired bodies, united in their worm-like dances, betraying their presence only by the stifled groans heard between the hoots of an owl. Was I ever that young?

As I drew closer to Barrymore the thoughts vanished. The house seemed larger, as it had appeared to me when I was a student, its ivy-smothered red-brick front and red-tiled roof standing vividly against an azure sky. Had it been a painting it would have been a still-life, for although life flourished within and around it, to view it from close by gave the impression of timelessness. It would always remain, even long after my own death.

Jennings was nowhere to be found. Somehow I had known this before even entering and yet, for the same reason, had passed through the motions of searching and of being surprised at his lack of presence. He would be, I knew, somewhere close, somewhere where he could find solitude and security, a place where the cringing terrors of reality could be dispelled, at least for a time.

And from somewhere within my own memories, I knew he would be in the chapel.

The interior was darkened, the only light coming from the outside, against the stained-glass high atop the building, and rimming the cloistered entranceway. The rows of wooden benches were empty, had been cleaned, Bibles neatly placed on shelves behind each. Yet the chapel felt filled, an invisible congregation in perpetual prayer creating a sense of power, a feeling of warmth. It was the perfect place to hide.

"Jennings," I said, my voice splitting the silence like a thunderclap. There was no reply. I looked toward the altar, at the huge organ pipes leading skyward in an artistic array of lengths, at the pulpit, elevated—the eyes of the congregation would have to look up at the priest—but there was no sign of movement.

"Jennings," I said again,"are you here?"

From above I heard a sob. I turned and stared at the loft behind and began to walk there. A small door led up a flight of steps to the loft. Quietly I ascended, stepped into the small area of it and noticed a hunched figure leaning against the wall of the balcony.

"Jennings," I said,"let's talk. It'll help." I put my hand

on his shoulder and he began to cry aloud, huge sobs wracking his body. He turned and held onto me tightly.

"It's . . . not . . . fair," he gasped. "It's not . . . fair . . . ."

"I know," I whispered, fighting to keep my voice steady,"but there are some things in this life over which we have no control. But we have to go on, let ourselves grow, live. You have to go on. Your parents would have wanted that for you."

"I want . . . them . . . back. I want them . . . to live."

"But they can't and you cannot change that. You have to accept what happened. Still, they will always be with you in your heart and in your memories. You have to go on, become somebody in this world, make them proud of you."

"You don't understand," he said firmly. He looked up at me, wiped his eyes with his sleeve.

I reached into my pocket and withdrew a handkerchief and handed it to him. He blew his nose long and hard, then wiped his eyes with it. "We were going to go to Switzerland for the term break," he said, flatly. "We were all going to go. I was really looking forward to it. My father promised that he'd teach me to . . . ski . . ."

For a time he just stared into the handkerchief as though it were a movie holding his attention. Then slowly, the sobs subsided, and along with it the sporadic hiccups of air.

"How do you feel?" I asked a minute or so later.

"Like it's just a bad dream. It can't be real."

I took a deep breath. "Perhaps it is just a bad dream."

"It's real," he muttered, unfolding the handkerchief and blowing his nose again.

"Yes. It's real. It's up to you now to go on," I said.

"I want to stay at school but I don't know if I'll be able to."

"Why not?"

"What if there isn't enough money for it?"

"There will be. The school has a policy just for that. They arrange with parents to ensure that there is enough put aside for the student to be able to stay. And if not, if there isn't, then they'll provide you with a scholarship, or something. But don't worry about it. You're a bright boy. There will be a way."

"It's peaceful in here. Sometimes I come here just to get away. You'll probably think that's crazy."

"No, I don't. I used to do the same thing myself. Are you feeling better? Just a bit?"

He nodded. "A bit. I don't know if I can go to the funeral, though."

"You'll be able to when the time comes. If you'd like I'll come with you?"

"That's okay. Would it be all right if I went to classes?"

"Sure. Whatever you feel most comfortable doing."

He stood up. "I'd better go, then." He began walking to

the door. "Thank you, sir." I nodded and he disappeared down the small stairwell.

"Jennings," I called out.

"Yes, sir."

"Come see me later on, all right?"

"All right."

I could hear the large wooden door open, noticed the brief pulse of sunlight fill the chapel before the door closed again. Then all was silent.

I could feel the tugging of the past inside me, saw brief flashes of light and color, the car and Solomon tumbling through the air, could hear sirens, that deep-tearing, wailing, feeling the terror pass through me, the thought that the body was dead, heard, again, the impact—was it a crack or a thud? And then I felt it fade. The darkness closed in around me, left me staring hard to see, left only flashes of light, pinpoints racing across the inside of my lid. So long ago. So long and yet still so fresh. But not just him.

My own life had upended. The memories gushed uncontrolled now.

And I could see myself standing in the morgue, staring in disbelief at the faces of the bodies of my parents that I had to identify, crying, wanting to hold them, be held by them yet knowing that it was too late for that. I would never be able to hold them again.

I stood up, felt my way through the darkness to the

door and hurried down the stairs and out of the chapel, into the blinding sunlight. I staggered across the small lawn by the cloisters and across the oval, toward the lagoon. My pace quickened as though I had been followed, and I knew that I had been followed, by something I could neither touch nor hold. I turned frantically, glanced back, then pushed forward blindly, stopping only when I had reached the row of birch trees bordering the oval.

I turned back, stared hard. I had to escape from the beauty, the perfection which never changed. I had to step away from the stillness, the death-like sense of self-betrayal; with each second my life was getting taken from me, placed within the buildings, the grouting between the bricks, the hair-like roots of the ivy adhered to the bricks. They were still with me.

I took a deep breath, rested against a tree trunk, and felt safe beneath the web of greenery. The peacefulness had settled in again. I stared with longing, wishing for a friend to come running by, to have something kind to say, or to see a girl that I had an infatuation for, to smile, an innocent, furtive glance, promising much. Both were missing, the track was empty, and the grass glistened perfectly.

"Out for a stroll?" a voice bellowed from behind. I turned, startled, yet recognized the voice.

"Smithers," I yelped. He frowned, looked hard, then casually smiled.

"Don't tell me," he insisted,"Wilson, it's David Wilson. I had heard that you were now among our esteemed ranks but I couldn't, for the life of me, remember what you looked like. Now it's all coming back."

"How are you, Mr. Smithers?"

He laughed, brushed his hands against his beard and said,"I don't think you need the formality now, unless you plan to enroll in my class."

"Of course," I said with a smile. "It's wonderful to see you again."

"And how are finding your role reversal? Settled in yet?"

"It's started quite fiercely," I told him. "One of my boys' parents were killed in a plane crash last night."

"Terrible business. I read about the crash in the paper just now. A terrible waste."

"Yes. I've felt awkward about dealing with the boy. I'm not sure what to say."

"It isn't easy. Don't think me rude, but if memory serves me, didn't your parents pass away while you were here?"

"Yes. Car crash," I said, feeling the control leaving me once again. "That was a long time ago," I hastily added. "A long time ago now."

"Yes, I'm sorry, I didn't mean to reopen old wounds, but I thought that you, above most, would know how the boy felt. Don't worry, David, you'll handle it just fine. Just fine."

I looked down. "I just don't know if I'm doing the right thing. It's not the same as before."

"You have to play it by ear. Gut feeling. Go with it and you won't go wrong."

"Mine tells me that I don't belong here, anymore," I suddenly told him.

"That's something that only you can decide. If you're having second thoughts let me assure you that it's only natural. Give it some time. Play the field. There's no urgency to decide. I remember when I first came here, I don't even remember the year now, but I had just arrived here from England and missed my family like hell. I didn't think I'd last a week what with all those stuffy-nosed professors still walking around with canes under their arms so as to be ready to dispense swift justice to those boys deserving of it. But I stayed. And I'm still here, even after all those old boys have long gone. The point is, give it a fair chance. For some it comes easily, but for others it takes a little time."

I smiled. "Thank you, I'll be sure to remember that."

"I've been here forty-two years, David, and they've been the best years of my life. I will miss this place."

"Are you retiring?"

"At the end of the term. It's been a long haul. I'm due for a rest."

"I'll be sorry to see you go," I told him honestly.

"Why? Because I'm the last of the Hitler-gang that taught you? Don't be. You've got a whole career ahead of you. Wait until you see the birdbrain they've picked to replace me. I doubt if he has the know-how to rub two sticks together and start a fire. But he'll need someone like you to show him the way."

"If I'm still here."

"You'll still be here," Smithers said, patting me lightly on the shoulder. "Well, I'd best be off before I catch something and retire prematurely. If you'd like, come by the house later for a drink."

"Thank you. I will."

Smithers began walking across the grass, slow, steady steps so as not to trip and fall. I watched him as he reached the road, stepping cautiously onto it, then again up the other sidewalk and into the Common Room beneath the clock tower. The glass door closed.

Above, I noticed the slight movement of the minute hand on one clock face. I remembered that no two sides ever showed the same time, or the correct time. I remembered climbing it for the first time, up an endless series of small steps, through the oversized mechanism, past the giant bell the next level up, and onto the roof, by the base of the flagpole. From there the whole school spread out, hidden from the rest of the city by the trees.

I remembered thinking how easy it would have been

to have leapt out and flown; the grounds seemed so perfect that even flight could have been possible. But the perfection had been in the buildings and the ovals and the warmth in those who had, at one time, passed through the hallways and the dormitories, and in those who were passing through right now. They were my charge now.

I reached down, plucked a blade of grass and slowly started my walk back to Barrymore House.

CHAPTER FIVE
ONE MOMENT IN THE SUN

"The real question is not whether life exists after death. The real question is whether you are alive before death."

~Osho Rajneesh

THE JERK who had just entered the coffee shop before us kept insisting that the door should be shut; a slight breeze was striking him on the back of the neck and this greatly upset him. It was an unreasonable request delivered as whiny angst. As it was the interior of the coffee shop was overheated and the slight breeze that filtered in through the crack of an opening was a welcome relief.

The others inside paid little attention to the man; they were the people still hung over from the night before having stumbled in to get some protection from the blinding light outside, or to eat the miserably cheap food to kill another hour of this drawn-out afternoon.

There were three of us, back then, who had walked in behind the whiner: Sam, Jess, and I, and all we wanted was some lunch, some privacy, and some way to spend the afternoon without having to think.

The whiner turned to Jess and again insisted the door be closed. Jess turned to Sam who in turn glanced at me, his eyes rolling skyward. I ignored the request as it was my misfortune to be wedged directly under the doorway; it should be my choice whether the door should stay open.

Moments later the jerk and his wife were seated at a table right by us. The waitress came over to them. Her name was Ruby and she had a wrinkled cigarette pinched between her teeth with a near-inch of ash hanging off the end. She was tall, her hair tied up, resembling the swirl of soft-serve ice cream atop the cone. She asked them what they wanted, but he only wanted the door closed; the breeze was bothering him. Ruby told him that she wanted to take their order, not hear their complaints. The jerk's wife looked at her husband hunched over in his seat, eyes scanning the menu like a vulture, fingers tracing the letters of the words by each item before he ordered. He had the wrong attitude for the place and also a lousy set of table manners. So they ordered the three-egg special and we watched from the door as Ruby left for the kitchen, her cigarette ash barely hanging on. The jerk turned his stare back upon us.

"Would you mind closing the door?" he asked again, more firmly this time. "The breeze is hitting me right on the neck."

"Certainly," I replied, neither moving nor intending to move. I minded, nor could I tangibly move. He stared for a moment more as if something would change, then turned to his wife and muttered something. She glanced up at us then screwed her face into a sour expression and muttered something back to him.

And then we were seated, the three of us, right next to *them*, and someone else took our place at the door, propping it open. He looked up at them and, after a few moments of deliberation, stood up and requested that *they* close the door because of the breeze.

"But we like the breeze," the man at the door said. “It's hotter than hell in here."

To this the jerk looked around the room, straight past us, and asked aloud: "Does everyone want the door open? Do you like the breeze?"

"Yes," we said in unison, and others in the place chimed in with the same answer.

"Then why don't you eat outside?" His wife muttered into her table napkin, unable to make eye contact.

"Then why don't you eat at home?" I countered to her which made her look even further away.

“A-hole," Sam muttered. "Such a jerk."

Ruby came over and took our order while we sat listening to the idiot couple's near-silent mutterings before starting up our own conversation. We sipped at the tepid water that had been placed before us then lit up our cigarettes, Sam pulling out one of his *Gitane* cloves, lighting up and letting off a billowing cloud of smoke above us.

"That's Venice for you," someone said from further back in the room.

The food came and by this time the jerk had nothing further to say. He was a fly in a coffee shop that turned out to be a flytrap. *That's Venice for you,* I thought, stuffing a forkful of eggs into my mouth and watching Sam and Jess do the same.

"Great eggs," Jess said. "I'll bet the chickens laid them like this."

"Imported chickens," Sam said.

Outside a cop car cruised by on the lookout for whatever it is that cops looked for in Venice. And on the beach in front, a small vagabond group stood, arms raised in the air, singing almost silently in front of a homemade sign which proclaimed: *Jesus loves you so much it hurts.*

A while later the jerk and his wife left. We applauded

them as they passed through the doorway, and someone shouted after him to close the door because they couldn't stand the breeze. We all laughed at that.

We were all flies in that coffee shop, small pieces of dust that had somehow been caught up, brought together for a moment, some as vagrants and some so hung-over that the coffee didn't taste like coffee, and the thought of eggs made them want to throw up.

But we sat there anyway, sheltered from a non-existent storm, imagining the steady dripping of water from the leaking roof. The Jesus singers continued out on the beach. They could have prayed for good weather, for all we cared; it was a Friday in 1980, and we were here to escape from whatever it was outside that we couldn't face. We were lost. Only we were not. We were some image of an avant-garde lifestyle we were not really living, students from a nearby college, fleshing out another weekend together.

You never know what you have until you lose it, I remembered thinking many decades later, those moments of youth when all things were possible, when you shone at your best, immortal, if only in your thoughts, with taut bodies, a full head of hair, and an athletic stamina that could drive sex for hours without a thought.

But the eggs were good, thick, not slimy, with a richness of yolk that coated the white toast dipped into it. Just like I did as a kid.

Sam had a mop of hair, tussled, not combed, a slight dimple when he smiled exposing a chipped front tooth. He had the slightest markings of a beard, without the thickness, which gave him that rock 'n roll look when paired with his black leather jacket.

Jess had a teardrop face, small pouty lips always painted bright red, mascara and dark eyeshadow, shoulder-length hair with lots of face-framing layers, and two thick eyebrows that gave her the look of a petite model. She also always wore a black leather jacket.

And I was tall and thin, over six-foot and just under a hundred and eighty pounds, more gawky than grace, insecure and yet caught up in this epitome of another life.

Those were my friends.

It was obvious we were done; words had stopped and we just stared at the walls waiting for Ruby to bring us the check. When she did we paid, each throwing in bills and coins, her tip included.

And we left, now a line no longer passed through that door, the earlier scene a distant memory. We headed further down The Boardwalk.

Oriental vendors hollered out their wares, all at the lowest prices possible. They promised a real steal, and much of it may well have been. There was everything from sunglasses to shoes, all in pretty little arrays, a vendor for every two square feet, it seemed.

I moved to one stall selling LPs, flicked through the

covers until I found a few that grabbed my eye: Vangelis' "Chariots of Fire" had just been a hit and the "Blade Runner" soundtrack was in demand, although Vangelis refused to release it. And here I held some of his earlier works, fresh to me, a steal to be had if I bargained well. I had a shitty turntable at the house, but this would still be a treat with headphones plugged in, so I negotiated hard, claimed the albums were overpriced and available further down for less and wound up saving a few dollars. Taking, the plastic bag with the three albums, I moved back to Sam and Jess. My music wasn't *cool*, but they said nothing. We all have our tastes and mine was a wide swath from Bowie to Vangelis—go figure.

Another time would find Sam and I doing our version of Michael Jackson's "Billie Jean" moves from MTV, as Jess watched and laughed at us. MTV was usually playing all the time. Cool was defined moment by moment. It could be anything.

But Sam was also driven by the guilt of turning down his father's request to mow the lawn, not that long past: the last thing he would say to his son. Sam told me this one day over a drink and a smoke. "I saw him out the window pushing the mower in the heat and he just fell down. And that was it."

I knew that guilt. I understood the power of that image, that emotion of the world dropping out from under your feet, beyond words and reason.

By the entrance to the liquor store a few doors down, two groups, one black and one white, stood together, quite obviously drunk, missing teeth with gnarled beards, dressed in torn army surplus clothing while one shouted milder obscenities to the other.

One approached from behind me. "Have you got a spare quarter?"

"Nope." I lied. There was no spare change down here, and no spare lives to be discovered in a small grotto café where jerks whined with their ugly wives while wasting an afternoon that could have been better spent sleeping. There was only a fluid motion, seconds slipping into minutes, into hours; an endless quagmire of human forms which never seemed to get anywhere, for no good reason. And the occasional cop car that drifted by observing, always observing, life on the other side of a fortune.

Slogans coated walls in black paint inches from beautiful and colorful, art murals, reproductions of street scenes minus the people. Only artists could appreciate the fine work put into them, could understand the ethereal value of these gutters and pool halls and bars where *family* remained a dirty word unless followed by a few drinks. But The Boardwalk was alive with characters you could barely dream into existence, rich, flamboyant people who could have come from traveling LSD roadshows.

One shirtless guy with a distended stomach was in a wheelchair. He looked like a Vietnam Veteran, a mad sparkle in his eyes as he wiped his sweaty forehead and wheeled into the bar where we were now drinking.

"Nice to see you here, babe," he said to every man, woman and counterpart that entered the bar. The guy with the Italian flair shrugged him off, nipping a cigarette from his own lips in a clean flash of motion. And then he was gone.

Belly rolled by, fighting to wedge his wheels through the bathroom doorway. But it didn't fit and he banged it into the frame, again and again, as though something would change, only it never did and you knew that he was going to go piss in the street now. But it was suddenly pouring outside and he might just as well have done it in his pants for all the effort would get him. No one would notice and no one would care. And he was gone leaving us to finish our drinks as the rain quickly subsided. It lasted no time at all, certainly not enough to disturb the street scene outside.

Just a few steps from the bar, a small fenced-in area allowed weight-lifters and bodybuilders to work out under open skies. A dozen or so of these *muscle bulgers* were there, and, as we got closer, we spotted among them, young Arnold Schwarzenegger, the *Austrian Oak*, a regular who had already made his mark and developed a decent-sized following.

This was the same teething ground for so many body-builders, past and future. Here Lou Ferrigno worked out his Hulk, with the likes of Jack LaLanne, Stanley Tookie Williams, Dave Draper and Bill Pettis whose claim to have the biggest biceps in the world bested even Arnold. And Joe Gold, the crusty Marine from East Los Angeles who brought Gold's Gym to life and into the iconic landmark it remained.

Arnold had just finished a set, now feeding himself with parts of a whole chicken along with a large beer. It took a lot to power that body. We meandered closer, Jess in the lead, edging her small body between people, passing guys who were staring at her ass, then at us as we followed like loyal subjects wondering what her next move would be.

Suddenly she leaned up, cupped her mouth and shouted out: "Arnie, I love you," and Arnold stopped mid-bite, wiping chicken from his boyish face, and focused in on hers, pleased by what he saw. Next to him, Jess was a small speck of a woman, however his eyes danced and he let off a large grin, the gap between his two big white teeth —monoliths on a giant's face. Only he wasn't a giant, standing at 5 ft, 10 inches, although he officially claimed otherwise. Still, his bulk more than compensated creating the illusion of a real-life Hercules.

"I like your jacket," he shouted back to Jess, his words thick with his Austrian accent, a slight nod of the head before he returned to his meal. It had been three years since "Pumping Iron" debuted. He was famous. It had been ten years since he first arrived in America at the age of twenty-one.

Jess turned back to us, pleased with herself. Others had noticed her as well, watching, uncertain how she knew Schwarzenegger, as evidenced by his reply. As she turned to walk out they cleared aside in a feigned celebrity reverence. Later, when I asked what she would have said if asked how she knew him, she said: "I'd have told them that I screwed him." This with a straight face, and I, believing that I knew her well, dismissed it only as fiction until I realized that her stare wasn't changing—she was good at keeping a straight face. And she was great with the BS!

A bare-chested white guy with stringy dreadlocks rollerbladed past us, his dog happily following on a short leash. To one side a Hispanic family was showering fully clothed by the wall.

"You never know," Sam said. "Friday is bathing day."

"You're such a shit," Jess told him, grabbing his hand and holding it as they walked ahead of me.

A frisbee flew across our path, and a scream came from the teen-girl who had carelessly thrown it; she ran after it oblivious to us, running as though she was dancing on tiptoes. On the beach where she came from, some hippies were molding sand into pyramids. I could smell the weed but couldn't see them smoking and couldn't tell where it was coming from. I inhaled deeply, anyway.

Just ahead we stopped. Sam leaned against a sidewalk post, pulled one of his *Gitanes* from the pack and lit it, its distinctive aroma wafting around us. Jess and I smoked Marlboros, me lighting hers before we both inhaled.

Behind us Arnold was bench-pressing again, his fan club loomed around him. He would be a "Terminator" in four years, although we didn't yet know it. And after that the "Governator" of "Kah-lee-fornia" as he would pronounce it. It was a crazy world.

"I like watching the people," I said to them. "I wonder about their lives."

"Like ants," Sam replied. "All just ants."

"They probably live here," Jess said.

I looked at her sardonically. "We live here . . . well, not on the beach, but not far away."

"It's not the same," Sam said. "We're young. We live free. We are artists."

"You play music," I said.

"You write," Jess responded.

"We all write," I replied quickly.

"Too cool," Jess said, inhaling and releasing a billowing cloud. "Too cool for our own good. I feel like getting drunk. Or high. Or both."

Another guy walked by with an ill-fitting Kay Baxter tee-shirt. It read: Voted Best Woman Body Builder 1979-1980. Kay Baxter wound up holding that title through 1984. Had he known he might well have taken better care of that tee-shirt. It could have been a collector's item.

"I want one of those," Jess said. "She's badass. We'll have to find a tee-shirt vendor that sells them."

Before we knew it was late afternoon and the sun was going down. The rain left puddles across the asphalt pathway. A new breed would emerge after dark, but for us we browsed a little further, scanning the rows of used jackets going for a buck a shot. We tried on a few, checked the pockets for loose change, then returned the jackets to the rack. We already had enough jackets for a lifetime. Enough to fit in anywhere.

"Would you do the same for me?" a girl in passing asked her companion.

"Hell, yeah," Sam and I both said loudly looking at her as though we'd been invited into the conversation. She gave us the middle finger and continued on her way.

Jess adjusted her shades. Sam adjusted his shades. I adjusted my shades. "We have attained anonymity," I told them. "Just three people roaming the streets."

"Three talented people," Jess said.

"Going places," Sam added. "Yeah, twenty-one and going places."

We turned the corner and came face to face with the cop car. We started to feign drunkenness, and staggered together to see what reaction we would get. One cop yawned. The other tapped his fingers across the steering wheel, waiting for us to get out of the way. No doubt their day was filled with images of stupid people.

Behind us the sun scorched the ocean, a fiery orange stained dirty black clouds above. Some vendors were packing up to go home; there's no way they would stay at night—too much of a steal to be had. Sometimes violently. After all, this was Venice, gangs and worse despite the new-wave cool and homeless-chic to be found everywhere.

Someone whistled at Jess.

"How much?" Sam called out, an impish grin across his face.

"Too little," Jess shouted out before the stranger had time to reply. "If that's what they think," she told Sam, "that makes you my pimp." We all laughed at that one.

But there you have it, we were out for a good time in a foreign land around the corner from where we lived on Rialto Avenue, with iron security bars on our windows and endless police and ambulance sirens that lulled us to sleep each night. It was all so abnormal that it was normal; we certainly didn't think otherwise. And we emerged into the light each day with the flies, vagrants, and jerks all wanting to close doors because of a little breeze; little cogs that made up the mechanism that ran the place. That ran our lives. Robots. Programmed. Not free at all. Barely cool enough.

And although we were young, we still scanned the

street for a touch in the right place, a nudge, a wink, a sigh. And although we were young, we didn't know yet that one of us wouldn't make it for much longer; that life was a breeze and you could only follow it so far before a door slammed shut; trying to make sense of a moment before it needed to make much sense. And all that could be had for the price of two fortunes. And all that could be had only once in a lifetime.

We headed home.

Thirty-six years and a divorce later found me at the entrance to The Boardwalk once again. It was December 12, 2016 and for some reason, I decided I should return for a nostalgic visit before the Christmas mania set in.

I was always like that, the one to cling to nostalgia, the last one to leave a school, a college, a life. I was the watcher, marking it all so that I could make sense of it, but really just catching the flavor like other people take Polaroids—well, before cell phone cameras and selfies infected the world.

Sam was now long dead. Jess was long gone, a new life on the East Coast, first with a record company, then her own band, before settling down, getting married, and becoming a teacher.

We spoke once, a few decades back after I had

scrounged up her phone number hoping to reestablish contact. And she seemed happy to talk, gushed about how we would never lose touch again.

"I love you," she said, over and over, but not in the romantic sense; rather as an anchor to the reality she once had and lost, unsure what else to say that could mean something relevant.

"Now that I have your number we'll never lose touch again," she said. "I promise." She was adamant about that.

And that was the last time we spoke, despite the advent of social media and the loss of privacy and anonymity. Maybe she didn't want to be found. Maybe I no longer wanted to look.

People make an impact on your life in ways you may not understand at the time. Some part of them stays embedded in your being, like a vibrant memory that holds an emotional feeling. And sometimes it's almost better that way, forever young, free of the tarnish of aging, or worse—a mundane existence.

I have no photographs of Sam—for some reason, we never took any, and yet I still see his face as vividly as that day on the Boardwalk. I still see those eyes that let you know you're a friend he's glad is in his life. It's a great memory to cling to. I still miss him.

As I stepped onto the path I could see the changes. New facades, paint, new structures. There were food vendors all over, many shops, still the murals remained, and that unique assortment of oddballs that seemed to forever roam the strip like errant cartoon characters.

Ahead a large sign proclaimed: Muscle Beach, and it was also emblazoned in huge black letters, outlined in white against the peachy-red building overlooking the area. Muscle Beach for weight lifters and body-builders had been upgraded. There was now a juice bar, among other things, and a more solid blue fence surrounded it, adorned at the base with barbell plaques immortalizing those who made the place; the great ones. The legends.

The crowd was larger, too, until I realized a film crew was there, camera lights jutting out from above people's heads.

There, by the fence, surrounded by adoring fans, stood the *Austrian Oak*, once again; Arnold Schwarzenegger, older, but still well-built. He sported a grey Tankfarm tee-shirt and blue shorts, supporting the barbell for a weight lifter in front of him.

I edged closer remembering Jess's trick from decades before. One of the other bodybuilders was holding an odd-looking green drink in a small glass and distracted me. "What's that?" I stopped to ask.

"A grasshopper shot, man," he told me. "All kinds of good shit in it . . . spiru . . . ."

"Spirulina," the cute blonde in the too-skimpy bikini standing with him said. "Phytoplankton, E3, wheatgrass, and cucumber. It's good. You should try one. " She pointed to the Muscle Beach Juice Bar just behind me with a flirty grin.

"Good shit," the lifter said, downing the drink, grimacing. I was not convinced. I edged further to the left, closer to Arnold until he was within earshot. Cupping my hands around my mouth I shouted out to him. "Hey Arnold. Jess says to say hello and thank you." I was doing my best to not laugh.

Arnold looked up at me, wiped some chalk from his hands as he thought of what to say back. Then he smiled, nodded, pointed at me with a broad grin. "Tell her I said hi back," he called out. "And she's welcome. Anytime."

Whether he knew it was bullshit or just knew what to say to appease fans, I nodded, glad that he had replied. Not bad for age 69, I thought. I gave him a thumbs up and shook my head with a laugh. *That* was cool.

I moved back and watched as he returned to his workout with the others once again.

"He comes here from time to time," someone on my right told me. "Still goes to Gold's. Cycles there. Hope I'm that good when I'm his age."

"Must be nice," I said absently, not looking at him, and edged further back onto the path once again.

For a moment I thought I should call Jess and tell her what I did, that same giddy sense of youth suddenly flushing back and infecting my mind. But the Jess I remembered, like Sam, lived now only in memory, frozen in time the last time I saw them both, a memory so bright that even thirty-six years later it all still seemed so real.

"And that's okay," I said aloud. "That's okay."

I turned back to where I had parked my car. It was already time for me to go home.

CHAPTER SIX
FIRE ON A DIFFERENT MOUNTAIN

JUST ONE MORE MOMENT.

The sky leaked, pale red pastels blending with orange hues as the sun fell behind the New Mexico hills.

They sat outside at Byron T's Saloon, the Plaza Hotel in the square, Las Vegas, New Mexico's quaint throwback to the old west. They'd been there for hours, the tall young man and his girlfriend; he was drinking heavily although he wasn't drunk, tequila shots with a Corona chaser, but she was sipping an iced tea, her belly large and round, her hands resting across it.

For a time they sat in silence. They were waiting the day out until the appointed time at 6 p.m. when they could leave, and the girl was already distressed and uncomfortable. Her hair, tied back loosely, no makeup, eyes reddened with tears, she fidgeted, often running her hand across her belly reassuringly.

"Are you ready for this?" he asked her, sipping at his beer.

"It's not like I have a choice." She wiped a loose strand of hair back. "You?"

"I guess. I wish it had been different."

"Do you?"

"Of course I do. We used to be happy."

"Happy! I've forgotten what that's like." She reached for her tea. "Will you be happy afterward?"

"For you. I want you to be able to move past this, have a life where you can be happy again."

She looked away at a line of smoke rising from the distance. The mountains seemed far away, not like the Sangre de Cristo chain behind the hotel. Her parents had moved up there, to El Porvenir, past the El Rito Cabins that local rancher, Tony Roybal had built, along the windy trail of the river amongst the pines and oak trees that littered the landscape, with the old Indian profile of Hermit Peak behind so prominently that it was staring at the sky above. She loved it up there, always enjoyed their visits—the sounds of the crickets, horses running through the fields, the powerful lightning storms that could appear as though an arms-throw away—although recently those visits had stopped; now it was all she could do to get out of bed each day.

"I packed your bags before I came," she told him. "They're by the door."

"Why?"

"After today you have no reason to stay. There's nothing holding you back and you know you want to be free of all this."

"I've stuck around this whole time. You're not being fair."

"You used to look at me. Your eyes were different then. You don't see me anymore."

"Lots of things were different then."

"Why couldn't they just take us this morning like they said? Why did they make this more painful?"

"They had a lot of babies today, the nurse said. It's not her fault."

"Save the defective mother to the end."

"Stop! You're not . . . ."

"You wanted a boy didn't you?"

"I just . . . ."

"What?"

"It doesn't matter." He took a swig of the beer almost draining the bottle. "We should do something for it, don't you think?"

"It . . . yes. I want to hold it." She leaned closer to him, her eyes brimming again. "I want it to know how much I loved it even though I couldn't make it live." She leaned back again and wiped her eyes. "I am defective."

"It's not your fault, Joy. They said it happens. It happens."

"But I had to carry it all the way. I wish I didn't have to."

"I know. It wasn't fair."

Next to them a couple with a dog finished up and left. They watched the dog, a retriever, as they all crossed the plaza square.

"Remember our high school prom? You looked so beautiful in your pink gown."

"Peach."

"Peach. Do you remember what we promised each other."

She looked at the ground and nodded.

"We still can."

"Can we? How do we do that?"

"I don't know, Joy. Your dad told me we shouldn't pretend about this. We should face it."

"My mom thinks we should move on, try again, even though they didn't want this for us. I don't think I could do this again, David."

He was about to reach for her hand when the server came out, a different one than the one that seated them.

"Hi guys. Michelle's shift is over so I'm taking over. I'm Candy. Can I get you another round?"

"Double shot, house tequila, and a Corona," he told her.

"Ice tea, please."

Candy nodded, smiled as she noted Joy's belly and clapped her hands. "When are you due?"

Joy stared at her, her face void of any expression. "Today," she replied. "It's dead."

Candy clasped her hands over her face in shock. "Oh my god," she blurted out. "I am *so* sorry."

"It's not your fault," he told her.

"I feel terrible. Please forgive me."

"Candy," Joy said. "It's fine. Honest mistake." But her eyes were sending the silly girl off to get the drinks and leave them alone.

"Another hour," David said, trying to break the mood. "What will you do tomorrow?" He knew it was a stupid question, but he didn't know what else to say.

"I want to change everything," she said. "I don't like the house. I want the nursery gone. Furniture. Everything."

He let her rant.

"Of course, I'll move after you're gone," she added. "Stupid for me to stay there . . . ."

"Stop saying that."

"It's true."

"You don't know that. You just keep saying it. Maybe you want me gone?"

"You don't know what I want. Just drink your booze." And it was true; he didn't know what she wanted.

Candy returned and quickly placed their drinks down, avoiding all eye contact and leaving as rapidly.

He downed his shot, then grabbed the beer and took a swig. "Do you still love me?"

"What?"

"You blame me for how things turned out."

"That's not true. It's just been difficult."

"It's been difficult for me too. Ever since you found out you've pushed me away, avoided me. I can't even touch you."

"I see the look in your eyes."

"What look?"

She sipped her tea. "We should go. It's almost time."

"It's early. The hospital's only five minutes away."

"I don't want to wait anymore." She banged the glass onto the table and covered her face. "It's been so hard waiting. Do you know I've been praying for a sign. Every day since we found out, I pray for a sign, just anything that it's still there."

"I didn't know you prayed."

"There's a lot you don't know. You'd be asleep and I'd go to the nursery, sit in the rocker and just pray and cry. But there were no signs. No kicks. No shivers." She wiped a tear from her face. "None of those things people with babies always say happens."

"I'm sorry."

"Why are you sorry?"

"I wish I'd known. There's no reason you had to be up by yourself. I'd have stayed with you."

"There's nothing you could have done."

"That's not the point."

He drank more of the beer, felt the cold travel down his throat. "The nursery was cute, wasn't it? The baby would've loved it," he said.

"Yeah. I remember how excited you were."

"I was." He was smiling. "It's funny, I didn't want to be a parent, you know? I wasn't ready. Until you got pregnant and it all changed."

"Do you think you'd have been a good dad?"

"I think so. Do you?"

"I think so. I guess we'll never know now." She clasped her hands together, raising them to her lips. "I'm scared," she told him.

"What about?"

"I'm scared when they take the baby that I'll die. I feel like I've died already. I'm scared when they show it to me because I'll know it's not alive." Tears were now freely flowing. She wiped at them and he got up to hold her, leaning over so he could get closer.

"I'll be there. We'll deal with it together." He reached for his beer downing the rest. He pulled a wad of cash from his pocket and counted it out, leaving it pinned under the salt shaker for the server. "C'mon. Let's do this," he told her, extending his hand for her to take.

"David, I just want you to know that I don't blame you. And I'll miss you. Us. But I don't blame you for that either." She looked at his face, searching for something she didn't know. Then together they walked to the car.

At the hospital, she was ushered into a birthing room and hooked up to an I.V. dispensing Pitocin to induce contractions and childbirth. The contractions came rapidly and quickly the nursing staff prepped her for delivery. There was no doctor present. None was needed unless there was an emergency in which case the doctor on-call would attend.

Legs up and spread apart, feet in stirrups, Joy was covered only by a thin, blue, paper gown. With each contraction, she began to groan, then cry. One of the nurses wiped her forehead and gave her some ice chips to suck on.

David waited until one contraction had passed, then moved so he was in front of her face and she had to look at him.

"I want you to know something. I love you. I love you and I don't want this to end here. I want us to figure it out together. I want us to try."

Joy reached for his hand and gripped it, starting to nod as another wave of pain overtook her.

"Bear down," the nurse said. "Push. The head is crowning. It's coming."

With another huge push, Joy screamed out. The baby easily came out and into the towel the nurse was holding. Joy was crying now. The nurse wiped the face of the baby, checking its genitals for a quick second before wrapping it up completely except for the face.

"Would you like to hold your . . . son?" she asked Joy, who nodded.

"Son," David whispered.

The nurse placed the baby on Joy's chest, waiting until she had a firm grasp on the baby before pulling away, allowing them their time. Joy stared at the little face, and ran her finger across the nose and lips. But there was no movement, no breaths, no cries.

She looked up at David and smiled. "I love you," she said. And to the baby she said it as well. "He's so beautiful, David. He's so beautiful. I couldn't love anyone or anything more." The wetness of her tears were now across the baby's face and she lightly kissed him on the forehead.

It was only when the baby opened his eyes and stared at her that she knew that everything would be fine, after all.

CHAPTER SEVEN
WORDS WITH SHARP EDGES

HE DIDN'T KNOW what to expect after almost eight years away. As the wheels of the giant jet touched the runway, his gaze was out of the small clouded window at the hills in the distance. These now unfamiliar buildings were not the Hong Kong he remembered.

His name was Charles Haddencourt, although his family had always called him Cheesy because he always smiled an overextended smile in all the family photographs. And yet, the irony was the English name was incorrect; a created name to accompany his Chinese name, Tâi Sún Huang—he was, after all, half-Chinese from both his parents, with a long familial history to go with it.

It was only after he collected his baggage and had passed through immigration and customs, exiting into the giant hall of the new airport, that he heard his sister calling him.

"Cheesy," she shouted, jumping up and down. His eyes had to adjust to the light, first spotting the slender teen jumping up and down, her ponytail bobbing from side to side. She was waving at him. With bags in hand, he nodded back. The last time he had seen her, she was ten. Her name was Lily—her Chinese name was Chéng Li, which translated to 'sincere' and 'beautiful,' something he could not deny; she had grown into a beautiful young woman.

"Chi chi," he said as he moved closer, "you've changed so much."

"And you, big brother," she said, leaning over to grab him, pulling him to her and squeezing him. "I'm so glad you're home." She let go long enough to duck under the rope barrier separating them and grabbed his bag. "Let me help you. Mother is very anxious to see you. She hasn't stopped cleaning since she learned you were arriving."

She steered him to an exit, motioning to a driver waiting to come to get the bags. "We have a ride home."

"The place does not look the same," he told her in the car. "I'm not sure I'd know my way around anymore." Then, staring at her intently, he asked: "Are you doing okay?"

Lily shrugged. "I still don't believe it. And then I do, and I cry." Her eyes welled up, and she hastily wiped at them with her fingertips. "Like now...don't do that...I'm trying hard not to."

"How's mother taking it?"

"She says nothing. She walks around and cleans. It's like she thinks that saying nothing means it didn't happen." Lily wiped her eyes again. "She's getting old, Cheesy."

"She is old," he said.

"No, I mean, she's getting old inside. She wasn't old before, but now it's like she became old overnight."

"This is a huge loss for her," he said.

"She's so happy you are here. Will you stay? For good?"

"What is the price for happiness? I will stay as long as I can."

For the rest of the ride, they sat in silence. The car meandered up Robinson Road; hairpin turns around fronds and thick foliage. Road signs were still both English and Chinese, but the traffic was far worse, with an endless line of taxis and buses competing for a single lane.

The car stopped briefly at the top to yield. This was the Peak area, the wealthiest of enclaves. They descended down one of the windy roads–no more than a wide footpath to his parent's house, a large three-story villa hidden behind a driveway. The house had balconies and terraces and a view of the harbor, an absolute rarity worth a fortune. From this height, he could see almost all the

Kowloon-facing side of the island—rectangular fingers of concrete and glass reaching to the heavens as though cut from a geode.

"Almost home," Lily told him. He snapped back from his memories and looked at her.

"More your home than mine, sister," he told her flatly.

"It doesn't have to be," she replied.

"Perhaps."

"He asked for you, you know," she said. "At the end. He asked for you."

"Did he?"

As the car pulled to a stop outside the front door, the servants came out, gathering around him, patting him enthusiastically on the shoulder, grabbing his bags, and taking them inside. Lily steered him forward, through the door, and into the lobby.

And there she stood, his mother, dressed in her usual black outfit, a string of pearls around her neck, and hair that had been freshly washed, neatly tucked into a bun. She stood hunched over, her eyes glittering, staring at him, a pursed smile breaking from her lips. On either side, a maid supported her, and balanced her as she wobbled closer to her son, grabbing his hands in her bony hands, and pulling them close to her.

"Hi, Mama," he said softly. "You look lovely." He held her tightly, his own eyes welling up.

"Such a liar," she admonished him with a grin. "I'm old

and wrinkled. But you look very healthy. I am happy that you have come home."

"Of course, I came. How could I not?"

She issued some orders in Cantonese to the servants that he did not understand—he never learned to speak Cantonese or Mandarin. He watched them scurry away, carrying his bags up the ornate stairwell, clutching the wide cherry wood banisters—the servants were not so young either.

"How are you doing?" he asked his mother.

"I'm not dead yet." He frowned when she said it, and she noticed. "I'm fine," she added, more adamantly, and her face lit up again. "Your sister has grown, eh?"

"She's a beautiful young lady," he told her, and the old woman smiled.

"Lily, take your brother to his room. I will have some tea put on and meet you in the garden when you're settled."

"Yes, Mama," Lily said obediently, grabbing her brother's hand and leading him up. "You have a new room," she added, "since you haven't been here forever."

On the third level, a room had been prepared for him. Lily pushed open the large door. At the foot of the bed was a small wooden chest. "Remember this?"

He stared at it, then nodded. At one time, it held his most prized possessions. He leaned over and opened the lid. And there they were, the comics that he had prized, repeatedly read over and over. "My God, she kept them?"

"Of course, she kept them. They were yours. There's more, but I told her we should start small."

"You're a kook, sister," he said. "Thank you for making me feel welcome."

"It's your home, too." She sat on the edge of his bed. "Mother said we need to order you some clothes."

"I have clothes."

"For the funeral," she corrected him. "Will you speak?"

"At the funeral? God, no. I should be the last person to speak about him."

"He was your father," she told him. "Of course, you should speak."

"I imagine he would not have wanted that."

"He loved you very much, you know. He couldn't show it, and you know that. Ever since Jimmy...."

"I cannot remember him ever showing it. That's sad, isn't it?"

She nodded. "I feel sad for you."

He opened his suitcase, flipping the lid back. A small wrapped gift sat on top, and he took it and handed it to Lily.

"Happy Birthday. Sorry, it's late."

She took it and smiled. "Only three months. Thanks." She ripped open the paper and pulled the necklace from within, a small diamond surrounded by a jade heart. She held it up. "It's beautiful," she said, then hugged him. "I love it. Help me clasp it?"

She turned around, extended the necklace around her neck, and allowed him to take the ends and secure them. Then she looked into the mirror by the door and beamed. "Where did you find this?"

"I didn't," he said. "I had it made."

"Wow. I love it. Thanks, brother."

"You're welcome."

Their mother was seated on a stone bench in the garden overlooking a small pond teeming with Koi. Around her, potted plants offered a color palette that made her seem regal. She smiled as they approached, and motioned for them to sit beside her.

"Settled in?"

"Yes, thank you. The room is very nice. I didn't know you kept my old things?"

"Of course, I kept them. I knew one day you would come home again." She patted his hand. "How is the family? My granddaughter?"

"Jess is fine, getting big. I brought some photos for you to see."

"And your wife? Is she well?" It was a question asked with no emotion behind it.

He took in a deep breath. "We're divorced now. We share custody of Jess. Jess wanted to come with me, but..."

"...but she would not allow it?"

"Something like that, yes. It would have wound up in court. There was no time."

"A shame. I would have liked to have met my granddaughter."

"Perhaps we can video chat with her?"

The mother seemed aghast. "Why would you scare her like that? I look old and wrinkled."

"You look fine, mother. You've always looked fine."

"Well, no matter. It is the way it is." She shifted positions. "Ah-Sook will be here this afternoon for a measurement. He said he could have the suit ready tomorrow."

"Thank you."

"You must be properly attired. Your father's business associates and our friends will all be there," his mother told him. "Will you speak on his behalf?"

"It doesn't seem right given..."

"I know it would have meant much to your father if you did so."

"What would I say? What a terrible son I have been! How did we not have a relationship? How it would have been better had Jimmy lived instead of me?"

"Do not say such things," his mother snapped at him. "Do not ever repeat such things." She stood up, took a moment to gain her balance, and turned to him. The maids by the door began to move to her, but she waved them away. "Your brother...we all mourn your brother, but we would never wish it the other way. And you are not a bad son. But you and your father are too alike, too stubborn, too much face to save. Despite that, he loved you very much. And I know you loved him as well." She moved to sit again, and he reached out to steady her arm. "As his son, you should speak for him. Take the time before the funeral to gather your thoughts and reflect."

"I'm sorry," he said. "I meant no disrespect to him."

"I know this," she said. "Sometimes a mother cannot say what she wants, must carry the knowledge of things she knows."

"I feel as though I do not know him enough to speak of him."

"And yet, you know him very well." She pounded a fist against her heart.

"I will try," he said.

She nodded. "I must rest."

He helped her up, and the maids came to help her back inside. He looked at Lily, who shrugged.

"I'm just glad I don't have to speak," she said. "I hate crowds."

Walking the grounds, he pondered what he would say as a eulogy. A father who would not hug his son for fear of feminizing him? Or the father, who was hyper-critical of everything the son did? He could not recall his father ever getting down to his level to play, talk, or goof off. Anywhere he needed to go, a servant was assigned to be with him; the father was too busy with his work, his investments, and his colleagues, always something critical that required his attention, something his son could not share with him.

One is not obliged to love one's parents because they are one's parents, he reminded himself. Every family must be a two-way street. Perhaps that's why there was no adult relationship.

Both his parents had not approved of his marriage. That was no secret. And yet they begrudgingly accepted his wife when they came to visit, at least until words were spoken and the trip ended rapidly. They left the next day. His wife swore she would never return, although she stopped short of asking him to stay away.

Nonetheless, he did stay away, telling his mother it was for the best, the father unable to treat him like an adult. After a year of near silence, he broke the ice with a birthday card, a letter, a call, ignoring the old man's stubborn refusal to meet his gesture halfway. His father would throw out words with sharp edges, statements almost designed to provoke, awaiting a negative response from his son. But Charles never responded, ignored each blade as though it had not been spoken, and ignored the pain he felt from them.

And time passed. Each year was a repeat, birthdays, holidays, end of the year. Each conversation was obligatory, with inquiries of health, weather, and plans.

Time passes like a thief, he thought. Eight years.

I don't know why I never brought Jess, he thought. His father had died not knowing his granddaughter. His mother was deprived of the joy she would have had. He told himself, *I am a bad son, just on that alone.*

He sat on the seat of a giant ceramic elephant statue, one of two that bordered the garden. He had spent many hours on these creatures in his youth.

"My father," he whispered to the air, "was a giant of a man. He commanded the sun and the moon and the very stars in the sky to do his bidding. Nothing could decline." But his father was not particularly tall, and he had outgrown him in height by the age of thirteen, a tall, lanky boy equally inexperienced as he was clumsy.

"My father could have been so much more of a father than he was," he whispered again, "and I could have been much more of a son than I was."

By now, it was getting late, and the sky had darkened. He could smell onions and leeks cooking, a familiar scent that wafted across from the kitchen above him. There, he knew, his mother would have instructed his favorite dishes to be prepared. These included chicken wings with mushrooms in a soy broth, steamed snapper with slivers of ginger with green onions, and cha tsu—barbecued pork sliced thinly, a savory sweetness in every bite. He was hungry.

When he arrived inside, the dining table had been set just as he remembered it. This included a place setting in the spot his father always sat at the head of the table. His mother was already seated, fussing over her lace napkin, smoothing the edges.

He walked over to her, leaned in, and kissed her lightly on the cheek. "It looks just as I remembered," he told her, moving to take his usual seat across from her.

"No," she said, her knobby finger pointing at the seat his father would have occupied. "That is your seat now," she said.

"Mother..." he began to protest. "It does not feel right."

"It is how it should be. Please."

He moved over and gingerly pulled out the heavy chair, pausing to study it. The chair was a dark cherry wood, firm seat, rounded back. The table was solid glass atop a cherry wood frame. He moved into position, sat, pulled the chair slightly, and then sat back and studied the table. "It feels strange," he said to no one in particular.

"Your father liked this table," his mother said.

"I just wish...."

"Wishing is a foolish game," she told him. "We all wish. Your father had lots of wishes that never came."

Lily bounded into the room. "Hey, family," she said. "Now, this is a treat."

"Be respectful, daughter," the mother instructed.

Lily stopped, bowed her head. "Sorry, Mama. I am just happy that my brother is home."

"As am I," the mother said. "But we must also respect why he is home."

Lily pulled out her chair and sat. "I know," she sighed.

The tastes and aromas of the meal compelled him to eat more, a richness he had missed over the years away. His belly felt full and warm. His mother was watching him, secretly delighting in his pleasures.

"Did you have enough?" she finally asked. "Have more."

"It was delicious," he said. "As good as I remember."

This pleased her, and she smiled and nodded, then slowly pulled herself to her feet, the maids rushing in to help her. "When you are done, please join me in your father's study," she said before turning and shuffling off.

Lily stared at him, and he at her. It was a mystery that would soon be solved. "Do you know what she's up to?" he asked.

Lily shook her head. "No clue. She doesn't tell me what she thinks, like I'm supposed to guess somehow."

"Mothers and daughters," he said with a wry smile. Lily glared at him.

"Fathers and sons?"

"*Touché*"

"Are you happy in America? Mother said you got divorced? Your choice or hers? And my niece?" The words came tumbling out, each pulling more with them.

"Sort of. Yes. Yes. Sorry," he said. "You know how

sometimes when you say nothing, after a while it is easier to say nothing than to say something? Or you say something, and your parents only hear what they want to hear, not really interested in the rest of it. I didn't mean to keep it a secret, but with things the way they were with father, I was angry."

"So what are you going to say about Father?"

His eyebrows raised in a question. "Father was a complicated man. When I was walking, I realized I only knew what he chose to share. I know where he came from, how life in Shanghai changed after the war, and how the family came to Hong Kong, but not about his life, how he felt, how he was as a young man. Did he have dreams about the future? What did he like to do? Why did he become so serious and so inflexible? Will that happen to me?" He stared hard into Lily's eyes. "How can you be related to someone and know so little about who they really were?"

"I guess that's true for most families. Parents have to parent their kids, not be their friends. Mother always says that she had to save for everything after the war, just in case it happened again. She never wanted her children to feel trapped without choices."

"Well, they were in a Japanese internment camp for almost five years. It can't have been an easy thing to live with, never knowing if something worse would happen.

The Japanese were quite unkind during the war, especially to the Chinese."

"And as much to the Eurasians, not quite Chinese and not quite Anglo. I can't imagine it. I tried making some family history, but no one wanted to talk about it. I know that our great-grandfather was buried in Shanghai, but they later dug up the cemetery to make way for an apartment complex. Mother says no one knows where he wound up after that."

He stood up to stretch. "That's why I never bother with the past. Everyone makes such a big deal about it, but at the end of the day, nothing remains of you, and eventually, no one is alive who knows anything. It's like you never existed."

She smiled at him and walked off. He watched her walk around the corner, her steps light and airy, as though she were a child without a care in the world.

When he was ready, he went to his father's study, sliding open the heavy door. The study was neatly organized, precisely as he remembered it. At the far end, his father's cherry wood desk, legs, and frame painted a traditional Chinese red, a black leather inset on top where his writing pads were. His silver fountain pen lay off to one side, and

Charles moved to it, picked it up, and opened it. The nib was gold, clean, glistening, and ready to be used.

Behind the desk were stacks of papers, investment account information, stocks, and beside that, a pile of correspondence; his father believed in letter writing, was not a fan of email or even of computers. But then, he was of a generation that had servants and assistants who would carry out his instructions. He never understood why that system was abandoned for the quick and easy modern way of doing things.

As a boy, the family would eat out at fancy restaurants. Thick linen tablecloths and wait staff that paid attention. His father hated how dining had become a crass exercise in indulgence; plastic tables hastily wiped, still smeared when you sat; self-service ordering from young people without any 'people skills'. "Why should I pay money for this?" he often complained.

Is that what happens when you get old? he wondered. The past goes away, and what you have left looks nothing like what you had?

He walked around the desk, pulled out the heavy chair and sat down. From there, he could see the whole study; the rows of books lining the walls—many were reference books or history books, but his father also enjoyed fiction.

His mother appeared at the doorway supported by her

two maids, just staring at him. "Sitting there, you look just like him," she said.

He stood up as she came closer, but she waved him to sit. One of the maids held a large package wrapped in brown paper and tied on all sides with twine. His mother took it from the maid and handed it to her son. "I know that you loved your father. I also know that he could not share with you what you are searching for. He was a very private man in that way. In the package are things that he never shared. A journal. This is a part of it. I have not read it because he never offered to share it with me. But you are his son. I think that it may be of some help to you as you choose the words you will say about him. I hope it will also bring some peace to you. Tâi Sún Huang, you are your father's son and will always be so. Remember that."

He took the package and set it on the desk, then walked around to embrace his mother. "I love you."

"And I love you. Ah-Fong will bring you some tea. I am going to retire."

He watched as they helped her out, and, for a long moment, he just stared after her. He could see the passage of her life slipping away. *One day she will be gone, and I will have lost all that I was,* he thought, knowing that he was not ready for it, hoping there would still be time left, yet knowing that it would not be that long at all. Such was life. You only appreciate things after you lose them.

He sat again, carefully unwrapped the package, and

found six thin hardback notebooks, each numbered carefully in his father's handwriting. His father wrote in small letters, carefully formed. He knew that the pen to his left had been the pen used as it had also belonged to his grandfather.

He chose one book and randomly opened a page, then stared at the date, frozen by it. It was the date of his brother's death. How could he have opened randomly to that page?

I grieve for the loss of my firstborn, James, whom we buried today. What crimes did I commit to be so cursed? No parent should have to watch their child wither and die, helpless to prevent it. What have I done to make the gods of our ancestors so angry with me to take him from us?

I watched his mother cry out in pain as his spirit left, her body wracked in pain that brought her to the floor. And the sound of her cries sliced through me.

Charlie and Lily do not yet know. They are safe with grandma for now, free from this sight. These past few months, so little time has been spent with them—all our strength has been with James. And now they only have each other.

I can do nothing more for James but honor him with a final ceremony. Can I even speak without breaking apart? What can I say that will have any worth against such a loss? All eyes will be on me. I am supposed to be strong. I am supposed to be of iron will and aged wisdom that can hold together my grief when all I wish to do is find a quiet place to grieve alone.

Charles put down the journal. He remembered the day well—how could he forget it? His father and mother sat with Lily and Charles after their return from the hospital. His mother could not speak, her eyes swollen from tears, holding her composure to not scare the younger children.

I remember my father putting a hand on my shoulder and the other on Lily's, he thought. "He's gone," he remembered his father saying, then wondering what he was talking about. *Who's gone? What is happening?* "Your brother is dead," his father added.

And that was it; no other explanation. His father hugged them both before taking his mother upstairs to rest. There was no family dinner that night—the kids ate alone. It was silent, not knowing what to say. The television was on. It was usually never on.

At the funeral, Charles remembered watching his father speaking. There was no sign of emotion, no tears—although his mother was visibly crying behind her black veil. His father spoke slowly, his words safe, kind, without a trace of grief that he had to have been feeling.

Now, reading the journal, Charles knew that the older man must have endured incredible pain to stand there like that.

It wasn't a coincidence that he had opened the journals at that page. He was sure of that. And although he would not have admitted it, he hoped that somehow his father had been guiding him. So he closed his eyes, leaned back, and randomly opened another page from another book. Then sat up, opened his eyes, and began to read:

I am at a loss for what to say to my son. He seems caught up in his anger to me. Have I not been a good father? Everything that I do is for my family, that they may have a good life free of the pain we suffered in our youth. With each word he recoils as though I were evil. It hurts me to see this, but I do not know what I can do or say to change it. To acquiesce would be to not parent well, and yet this, too, is no solution. He is particularly hard on himself. Wrapped up in his comics, he seems far removed from reality as though somehow that is a solution. Do I strip them from him? It seems that is his only solace, so I say nothing. It is my wish that we spend some time together, but I can find no activity that he enjoys. I am at a loss.

The journals shook him. This was a father he never knew, one who would never share his feelings with his son. And yet, too, there was a familiarity in reading them; this man was not that different from himself, caught up in all the conflicting emotions that seemed to have no answer. He wished that his father was alive to at least share some words now. *But that's life's cruel irony*, he thought, *never in time, always too late. Things unsaid and left undone.*

In the study alone, he spent most of the night reading through the journals, stopping only to contemplate his understanding of them before reading them over again. He read through the stack of letters that had been sent to him, again finding threads of his real father in everything. At four in the morning, he retired to his bed, falling asleep with his head filled with the words his father had written.

Even in his dreams, the words came to play, filtering through him like shards of light reflecting off anything it came into contact with.

And then *he* was there, standing before him, his father, tall, dressed in the suit he loved. And again, Charles was ten, looking up at his father for some sign of affection.

"I'm sorry, father. How could I have known?"

His father walked closer to him. The older man's face seemed somehow softer. He put his hand on Charles' shoulder.

"I too, my son," he said. "Foolish pride prevented me from showing you. But now you know."

"What changed? While Jimmy was alive, you were different."

"When James died, I could not express the pain that I

felt. No parent should ever lose a child. You spend your life being strong, protecting your family, only to learn that life can be cruel and take them from you. Watching James die, we only wanted to protect you. But I could not believe that life could be kind anymore. It had stolen one son, and I did not want it to steal another. I had. to be sure."

"I wish you could have told me these things," Charles said.

"We are both stubborn, my son. Perhaps in too many ways, we are alike. Your mother always said so."

His father turned to walk away.

"Please stay," he called out to his father. "Just for a minute more."

The old man turned back. "We are always together, my son. This is *your* dream, remember?" The man smiled.

Charles awoke in his bed. It was morning, and sunlight was spilling into the room. He rubbed his eyes, still groggy.

After he was showered and changed, he went back to the study and sat back in his father's chair, his hands gliding over the journals spread out in front of him. Then, from the top desk drawer, where he knew it would be, he pulled out several sheets of paper and placed them before him. He opened his father's fountain pen and brought it over to the paper. Carefully he began to write, the letters small and distinct. It felt quite natural.

"My father was a complicated man," he read aloud as

he wrote before continuing silently. He was so intent on the task that he failed to notice his mother at the door peering in. She watched him for a moment and smiled as though he had always been there, or perhaps that the son had become the father and the father the son, both united now in this one task. She moved off. Shortly, some food was brought to him, but this, too, he failed to notice.

He failed to hear Lily when she bounded in, instead focusing on the words that now flowed with ease. She circled behind him and glanced at what he was writing, making out only a few words here and there... "rich from the pain that...."

Since he was not responding, she left him alone, found her mother in the garden, and sat beside her on the bench.

"Have you seen Cheesy today?" she asked.

"He is busy with your father's eulogy," the mother said with a smile.

"You're smiling," Lily said.

"Your father would be happy to see this," she said.

"It's nice having Cheesy here. Do you think that he will stay?"

The mother patted Lily on the cheek. "His life is not here, daughter. He is also a parent. But perhaps we can see more of him now that he has come home again. Perhaps you and I can even make a journey to see his life."

"I'd like that," she replied. “But why did he think father didn't love him?"

The old woman laughed. "Men are very simple creatures. They only know two things: they go, or they stop. Women help men to find other things, to go slow, or to stop and look. It takes a strong woman to make a man stronger."

"Isn't that kind of sexist?"

The old woman laughed again. "In our culture, it has always been like that. The man is important, and the woman beside him is silently important."

“I like hearing your stories.”

"Old stories?" the mother asked. "Very old stories."

"You should tell me more."

"I will, daughter."

In the study, Charles continued with the eulogy. Throughout the day, the words flowed. More food was brought in and removed, and sometimes he would stand to stretch.

Often he would mutter to himself or to the memory of the father he felt standing with him. The people who would be at the funeral had known his father far longer than him. They would also know that he had been an absent son, and might consider him an inappropriate choice for the eulogy.

He pushed the thoughts aside. It was what his mother wanted. And if she was to be believed, it was what his father would have liked as well. He emerged briefly only for the measurements the tailor required for his suit.

Finally, when all the words were exhausted, he placed the lid back on the pen and put it exactly where it had been. He sat back in his father's chair and took a deep breath. The eulogy was good. It was fair and just and, he hoped, captured both the father and the son. Of course, time would tell. Outside the light had started to dim.

Ah-Fong entered the study with a glass of Scotch, and a single ice cube in the glass.

"Sir, always enjoy Scotch after work," he said, placing a coaster on the desk and the glass after it. "Ma'am says to bring it to you." He turned and quickly left.

Charles lifted the crystal glass, swirled the liquid, and sniffed at it. He wasn't a big drinker and likely couldn't tell a good Scotch from a low-grade Scotch. Taking a sip, he placed it down, held it in his mouth, and then swallowed. It burned as it slipped down his throat. For a moment, he could almost hear his father sigh.

"We shall see, father, how well this goes." He gulped down the rest of the Scotch and firmly placed the glass on the desk.

The morning of the funeral arrived. His father had made all the arrangements years before, sparing his wife the pain of handling it. The mortuary brought the closed casket and placed it upon a stand in the garden; his father did not believe in seeing the made-up remains. His father believed that the fact of death itself was closure enough.

Alone, Charles paced around the coffin. At one point, he gently touched the top of the polished wood, then continued out to the front, where guests were arriving. With so many people and nowhere to park, most came with a driver or by a taxi, dropping them off and clearing the driveway for the next. Rows of chairs had been set up close to the coffin. A small podium had been placed in front.

His mother and sister were already by the door, greeting guests. He approached them, eyeing the growing crowd, all unfamiliar faces. As they greeted his mother, then sister, they shook his hand, and muttered words Charles did not hear, his mind still wrapped in the eulogy and his ever-growing fear that he might fail his father once again.

"Thank you," he would automatically respond to whatever had been said, then again to each that passed him. Finally, the guests had all arrived, and the family took their seats at the front.

The director of the mortuary took to the podium.

"Good morning. My name is Kam Fong Lee, director of Pleasant Valley Mortuary. I would like to welcome you all. I have been asked to let you know that following this memorial, the family will proceed to private cremation. They thank you for coming here to pay your respects to their loved one, Sún Bo Huang. Honoring his father, esteemed son, Tâi Sún Huang, will first share his thoughts.

Lee gestured at Charles to step up. Charles looked at his mother, who nodded her support. Lily patted his arm. He rose, adjusted his suit, and slowly approached the podium.

For a long moment, he surveyed those who had come, knew them to be family friends, business acquaintances of his father, as well as distant family members, most of whom he had not seen since he was a boy.

"Honored guests," he began, his voice slightly wavering. "My father was a gentle man with the heart of a lion. His humble origins in Shanghai, where he met my mother, and his dedication to his family, brought him much success despite the struggle of internment during the war."

He took a deeper breath. He could feel a calmness settling over him.

"My father was a giant of a man, at least to me. Growing up, I was in awe of his stature, certain that I could not reach the level of success, both personal and business, that he had. A son always greatly feels the shadow of the father, no matter the relationship."

Now he could feel a warmth he had not expected. It comforted him, like a hand upon his shoulder gently guiding him forward.

"To stand here today and honor my father before you has humbled me in ways I never imagined. You see, despite the strengths of my father, he always did what he knew needed to be done for his family. Even when it created friction between us.

"My father was not my friend. This is unlike what we see in the world today, where parents seek the approval of their children and ultimately fail to raise them properly as respectful adults. My mother reminded me recently that a parent's job is to raise a child so that he or she can be independent, strong, honest, loyal, kind, and hopefully intelligent."

There were some chuckles from the crowd, quickly suppressed so as to maintain decorum.

"I have been fortunate to learn of my father's private thoughts and through his writings to better understand the powerful image of him from my youth compared to the reality of who he was and the burdens he carried alone. And while I cannot share these personal details with you, I can share that my father, like all men—and any who deny this are not truthful—held the same fears, doubts, and worries that all parents feel, striving to find that fine line between doing the right thing, saying the right thing, and showing the right thing. And somehow still being able to live a full life. A son only sees what his father chooses to show to him."

He paused for a moment, his eyes scanning the faces watching him. He saw many subtle nods, some smiles, and some tears. But, too, he could see eyes riveted to the words he was saying.

"My father cannot be judged for any failings I might have perceived of him in my youth or any that others may have perceived. For we are judged by the constancy of our actions, not the accuracy of our choices, for the strength of our heart and not errant words that may occasionally emerge. We undertake this journey together, even when we are separated by distance and time, for the bonds that tie us are strong even when we think we cannot see them. This is why we are family. And that is the lesson my father always worked to teach. No, he was not my friend. He was far more than a friend could ever have been. He was my father, always, even now, in death, until my own last breath, for he lives within me now, just as I was within him while he lived. No matter the distance."

He adjusted his tie and took a slight pause.

"My father was a great man, a careful man, a considerate man. And like his father before him, he did the best he could do in all things. If I can be half the man my father was, I will have escaped the shadow of his stature that I so long feared and will find myself basking in the light of the many memories I now hold dear. I offer now far more than just respect to the life of my father...."

He stopped, his eyes welling. With a handkerchief from his breast pocket, he lightly dabbed the corners of both eyes before returning it.

"Thank you father. With pride, I shall always be your son."

Charles stopped, and folded his notes, his eyes looking at his mother and sister, both crying freely. He stepped down from the podium and walked to them. Both rose to embrace him.

"Beautiful words, my son," his mother whispered to him.

"You did it, Cheesy," Lily told him.

He sat motionless, could feel the tears brimming again, ready to burst, but he held his composure the way his father would have.

He sat still as others in attendance rose to speak of his father. He listened to their words and understood them in a new context.

Afterward, as those attending paid their respects, he was taken aback.

"Your father spoke so highly of you," one said.

"Your father often spoke of the pride he felt of you," another said.

"You remind me of your father very much," yet another told him.

"Thank you. Most kind," he replied, his mind on fire from words he had not expected to hear but happy to hear them, nonetheless.

"You are your father's son," another said.

"Excellent words," someone else said. "Is there a written copy I may borrow to read again?"

The eulogy had been written in pen, small distinct letters that looked just like his father's handwriting. *Funny*, he thought, *I never used to write like him.*

After the guests had all left, it was just the three of them again. Before they would journey to the crematorium for the final goodbye, they shared some Jasmine tea in the garden as workers removed the chairs, restoring the area to how it had been.

"Your father would have been proud of you," his mother said.

"After reading his journals, I feel I understand him in a way I never did before. I'm sorry for all the years I never came," he told his mother. "It all seems foolish."

"I know," she said, patting his leg. "What will you do now?"

"In a few days, I'm going to go back home," he said.

His mother's eyes dimmed just a bit, enough to be noticed by both her children. "But only to arrange it with Jess's mother to bring her back with me and spend much-needed time with you. It's time she knew her Hong Kong family."

"I'd like that," the mother said. "I'd like that very much."

And her eyes came alive once again.

CHAPTER EIGHT
THE DELEGATE FROM MARS

"HE WAS VERY GOOD-LOOKING." Cassie Michaels, an aide to the delegate from Brazil adjusted her hair as she looked directly at Jason Fila from Channel 2 News. "That was the first thing I noticed." She was smiling, almost breaking into a schoolgirl giggle, covering her mouth with her hand for a moment before continuing. "I don't think I was the only one to notice," she said softly.

Jason looked at the camera, his face a "shoot me" expression. *Fifteen years a reporter for this*, he thought. But he was professional enough to know he needed to press on past this point.

"What else?"

"He had a lovely British accent."

"British?"

"Oh yes, a sophisticated accent, classy, intelligent."

"Intelligent?"

"Yes, you know how British people always sound highly educated when they talk?"

"Isn't that a bit superficial?"

"I suppose," she said, running her fingers through her hair, twirling a strand at the end.

"But you were not afraid?"

"Afraid? Oh no, not at all." Her voice had taken on a lyrical charm. "All he did was talk about the problem and how it needed to be fixed."

"In a British accent?"

She giggled now. "Exactly."

Three hours earlier:

The spaceship against the New York skyline was immense, its length exceeding that of Manhattan Island as it settled and stopped over the city.

There had been no dramatic overtures, no flaming clouds roiling ahead of its approach—this wasn't the movies, after all.

Below the city slowed to a crawl, onlookers focusing skyward. No panic. The arrival had been announced across all major media despite a gag order from the White House.

A full assembly of the United Nations had been called into an emergency session. This too had been requested.

The leaked message read:

Don't be afraid. We come to talk to you. This is not an invasion. We request a full assembly of your United Nations tomorrow at two in the afternoon, your fourteen hundred hours. Our delegate will come to speak to you. He will be unarmed. After discussion, he will leave in peace, as will we. Thank you for your attention to this matter.

The message had been unsigned.

While the military scrambled, the great ship simply hovered, blotting the sunlight from the ground beneath it. There were no exterior running lights—why would there be? High-speed space travel would make such things redundant. The exterior was smooth, metallic, devoid of apertures, gun turrets or any markings. It was one uniform shell, smooth and light grey.

At two the next afternoon a huge crowd surrounded the U.N. building. The military had established a perimeter leaving a single entry checkpoint for the delegate to enter.

Media across the planet were primed, multimedia trucks jammed tightly together, cameramen and equipment atop the roofs, all gear pointed to the entry point. A myriad of talking heads was killing time before the main event, endless hypotheticals ungrounded by any facts.

Inside against the back wall the scene was the same. Armed military personnel stood on guard. The Secretary General, Kurt Schleiger walked up to the podium and motioned the group to quiet down.

"I call this meeting to order," he said. "This is an exceptional day for humanity. Long have we searched the skies asking if we were alone. Today that question has been answered by our visitors. I urge restraint from the floor. I urge restraint from all governments to not rush to any military action. Let us listen to their delegate and hear their message. Hopefully, we will also be permitted to ask questions." Schleiger tapped his earpiece. "I am told the delegate is entering the chamber." He motioned to the back wall.

All cameras swung around. The doors were opened by two military guards and there stood a tall, very human form. Dressed in an Armani suit, he started down the aisle toward the podium.

And then the delegate from Japan stood and began to applaud. Soon the assembly all joined in, sustaining the applause as the delegate ascended the steps to shake the hand of the Secretary General before facing the audience.

The delegate had thick, lustrous black hair, cut neatly and swept back. His eyes were a piercing cobalt blue and his skin color a neutral tone, neither too light nor too dark.

Depending on what angle you looked, one might see a different shade. He was lean, yet muscled, evident in his hands as he raised them to motion the crowd to be seated.

"Thank you," he said. "My name is Viet Quora." He had a strong British accent, vowels well formed and his inflections precise. The audience hummed with speculation. He waited for it to stop. "I come to you as a representative of my home world, a planet you call . . . Mars!"

The chamber erupted, delegates conferring with each other, the statement they had just heard made no sense to them. "But he looks so...human," one voice shouted.

He waved them silent.

"Yes, I did say Mars, a planet you consider lifeless save for a few microbes here and there, with no sign of civilization past or present and insufficient water to sustain life without major terraforming." He took a breath. "All I can tell you is that you are wrong."

Above him high-definition, holographic images appeared, a video of imagery showing a vastly different red planet, one with blue skies and sweeping vistas of green, and tall crystalline spires pointing to the heavens, glistening as jewels. Another angle showed crowds of ordinary-looking people in ecologically balanced communities, hover cars, and lush vegetation from every opening.

"Our two worlds are sisters, formed at the same time, four billion years ago by your timekeeping. Both have seen rises and falls in civilization. The primary difference is that our world, unlike your own, does not have a history of strife, dissension, and unremitting warfare."

The images faded out.

"How did we escape detection, you ask?" Viet nodded, mildly amused by the tale he was about to tell. "At first it was not difficult. In your year 1600 as telescopes were first pointed our way, we simply wrapped our planet in a holographic shield preventing you from seeing anything more than a fuzzy red ball. And for many years that sufficed. We went about our business and you went about yours."

"What changed?" Schleiger asked from the side where he had been standing. Viet looked at him, reminding himself to overlook the rude interruption. Instead, he motioned Schleiger closer, deciding to use this man for questions rather than allowing a general shouting out that he found distasteful.

"My dear sir," Viet said, his accent clearly pronounced. "You changed! Between wars, your technology improved. Your telescopes improved until finally, you placed Hubble into orbit offering you superior imagery and forcing us to step up our game." He waved his hand across the audience. "Between your 1964 and the present you've sent continuous waves of probes to our planet in the hope of finding life of some kind. The only problem is...we do not wish to be found."

Again the assembly erupted into side chatter, the hum

increasing until Viet raised his hands high and swept them back down. "Early on we just destroyed your probes before they entered the atmosphere. When it became evident you would not stop we decided to give you what you wanted."

"What do you mean by that?" Schleiger asked.

"We allowed your probes to land, Viet said, his eyes studying Schleiger. *Just like all humans,* he thought. "We knew exactly where they would land. In the event the landing would impact a city, we merely offered you technical difficulties and adjusted the site to suit our needs. There we erected a containment field, a projection of a barren landscape, sterile soil samples, and sterilized rocks. After a reasonable time frame, we disabled the probe. We have quite a collection of your probes in our museums. We hoped that if you found a dead world you would cease your visits. Sadly this was not the case."

Viet moved to face a different section of the assembly.

"Your probes became more functional. You sent rovers and so we had to adjust the landing area to accommodate a far more complex deception. The rovers would emerge onto a moveable base. Before the signal with Earth was established we had already plugged into the device to feed holographic information directly to the rover's computer system. While it appeared to be traveling across the face of our world, your rover was, in actuality, stationary, feeding you three-dimensional imagery with a three-hundred-and-sixty-degree landscape." Viet brushed back a loose strand of hair and smiled, tilting his head slightly. "It still is!"

"Amazing," Schleiger said.

"Truly," Viet responded. "One of our more detailed efforts. You have no idea how difficult it is to get an entire population to be silent for the quarter hour needed to access the rover circuitry. But there you have it."

The crowd was buzzing again. Viet again raised his hands so he could continue.

"Please do not misunderstand our actions. Our intentions are not meant to be hostile. *You* invaded *our* world. All we want is to be left alone in peace."

"Will you accept questions from the assembly," Schleiger asked.

"Within reason," Viet replied. Hands immediately shot up.

"Mr. Kent, the United Kingdom delegate," Schleiger announced.

Kent stood, a stout man wearing an ill-fitting suit and sweating profusely. He was handed a microphone. "Thank you," he said, "and welcome to Earth Mr. Quora. I have two questions if I may. First, why the British accent when you clearly are not from the UK? And second, why hide from us at all?" He handed the microphone back and sat.

Viet was nodding. "Absolutely," he said. "Good questions. The first. From our studies of your world, we have learned that your race infers intelligence based on audio presentations. An example of this: two men, identical in every way, both—as you call them--black men, one speaking in an urban street dialect while the other in an Oxford tongue. Remembering that I said they are identical in their intelligence, however, the one with the British accent is considered intellectually superior. It is a ridiculous simplicity, however, we wanted to make you feel comfortable, that we were not a threat and the accent sufficed for that. For the record, I have no natural accent."

The crowd was buzzing again. "The second question: why hide from you? It should be clear to you that our two societies are polar opposites. While we've maintained peace for hundreds of thousands of years, you've engaged in endless warfare, blaming each other for any and all failings as a whole whether an ideology or political conflict. You are incapable of peace. Furthermore, you have polluted your oceans, and your atmosphere to near toxic levels, with everything from chemical to radioactive emissions in pursuit of profit. All aspects of your commerce is wrought with substandard materials and inflated costs with a monetary system that places value of attainment rather than achievement. Your governments and political parties across the spectrum are corrupt and fail to serve the very people they were meant to represent."

Now the room was silent and he knew that he had

struck a nerve. Nonetheless, they needed the truth and not some pasteurized version of it. He swept back another strand of hair and went on.

"How would an association with you be of any benefit to us? Every peaceful indigenous society to have lived on this world has been wiped out by the present dominant society. This includes the Aboriginals of Australia, the Indians of the Americas, as well as in Africa, Asia and Europe. Who knows of the Yuki, or the Palawan or Herero tribes? We view this as an endless genocide simply because your prevailing attitudes refuse to coexist in peace. We cannot allow that into our society. Will not! And yet we do not force our views upon those with whom we disagree, just as we will not force your society to change. A common English axiom, I believe, states that just because you *can* do something does not mean you *should* do something."

"Mr. Zerinski, the delegate from Russia," Schleiger said.

"Thank you, comrade," Zerinksi said. Like Viet, he was tall and slender, almost equally well-dressed. "Are you saying you wish no contact from us?"

"That is *precisely* what I am asking," Viet said, stressing the word 'asking.'

"And may I ask how you plan to prevent us from exercising our right to explore Mars?"

Viet wagged his finger at Zerinski. "Also a good question. "*khoroshiy vopros, comrade.* We are not violent and we will certainly not attack you. So let me be very clear. We will not tolerate further attempts to land on Mars without our permission, permission, I might add, that we will not be giving at this time. Mars belongs to *us*, period!"

"Isn't that unfair?" The French delegate shouted out. "Surely there must be a compromise we can reach?"

Viet shook his head at the man. "Pas de compromis—one only compromises when one wants something. *Nous ne voulons rien de toi.*"

"And how, for argument's sake," the Russian delegate also shouted out, "will you stop us if we choose to continue?"

The floor cheered him on with numerous shouts of "yeah."

Viet took in a deep breath and look up at the ceiling for a moment, recognizing the swell of attitude he'd come to expect from this breed of humanity. "We are quite prepared to stop you," he replied without the slightest tone of aggression in his voice. "When I tell you, as I have come to do, that this is not an option, I would expect my words to be taken seriously. My coming here was strictly a courtesy."

"Your coming here and talking to us as children is an insult," someone else yelled from further back.

"No!" Viet said loudly. "You are not our children. But we are related. Four hundred thousand years ago, a branch of our people, choosing not to abide by the standards of peace that we established, left our world for yours. At the time primitive hominids roamed the planet. Our ancestors set up their own civilization, blended and even mated with the local peoples and *you* are the result of that. For whatever reason, those traits have rooted into the very fabric of your being. This is unfortunate. One day perhaps, when you have shed this aspect and can live in peace, we may welcome you back. Your space travel is still in its infancy. Our worlds pass twice yearly in their apogee and perigee. Trust me when I say, we *can* ignore each other." Viet shook his head. "Thank you for listening to me today."

Viet bowed slightly to Schleiger then turned to leave.

"And if we don't?" Asked the Secretary General, his voice uneasy and quiet.

Viet stopped and turned back to the podium, his eyes fixed on Schleiger. *The man was already an irritant*, he thought. "If you choose to disregard this request we will be forced to take drastic action. We have already calculated and prepared for this eventuality, although we hoped that it would not be forced upon us. But, very well." He inhaled deeply, the differences in the quality of the air quite apparent to him. "We will preserve our race at all costs. If this requires moving our planet *out of orbit* to a nearby star cluster where we can safely insert it into a new orbit, so be it! We *can* do this safely. For you, however, the loss of Mars in its present orbit will impact your own orbit, drawing you closer to Sol and negatively impacting life on your planet, more so than that which you have already done. It could, potentially, be an extinction-level event for Earth. This is not our wish. All we ask is that you leave us in peace. Explore other planets in the system."

"You would do this to us?" Schleiger asked.

"It is not our choice, sir. The choice remains with you."

"Will you allow us to contact you? Advice? Guidance, perhaps?"

"We will be watching your development. Change must be your own and we cannot guide you. To coin your own phrase, sir, don't call us; we'll call you." Viet bowed again to the man and began to stride up the aisle. At the back of the chamber the guards, still in shock, opened the doors for him to pass through before closing them again. One guard tapped his earpiece to let exterior security know that he was coming.

Outside, the noise dropped away as they waited for Viet's appearance. He had not been spotted entering and it now seemed a long time for him to emerge. When it became apparent that he would not be coming, the reporters began to break down their equipment. "Did he beam out or something?" one asked.

As the other delegates slowly emerged, Jason Fila

spotted a pretty young woman among them. He quickly approached her. "Miss, Jason Fila Channel 2 News, may I ask you about what went on inside?"

The pretty brunette smiled and nodded.

"What's your name?" he asked.

"Cassie Michaels," she told him.

CHAPTER NINE
CEREMONIAL

LILIES.

The room burst with lilies from vases to planters, poised so that no table, no surface, was left empty of the slender flowers. The lilies matched the embossed lily on the invitations, a tincture of azure lining the crease along one edge of the embossing.

The rest of the room lay darkened, walls lined with tables and food stacked upon metallic warmers awaiting the reception, their succulent contents emitting a taunting aroma of stew, lamb, prime rib, shrimp, and every other imaginable culinary delight.

Aliajandra just loved the receptions. Dressed in a fine satin gown, she held her seventy years with pride, flawless in her appearance: cultured pearls just balanced enough to compliment her neck now that she had recovered from the surgery and could happily display her neckline again. She had lost count of how many of these ceremonials she had attended. Since they had become the accepted way of life, it seemed as if a week didn't pass without at least one person taking the affirmation and entertaining with a grand reception like this one; after all, it was paid for by the State.

Aliajandra loved lilies. She fondled the embossed lily of her invitation, her index finger with her three gold wedding rings, gently caressing the outer lips of the printed flower. This ceremonial had particular meaning for her; this was for Billy, her darling Billy whom she had bounced upon her knees all those years ago. It was a shame his mother, Jacquelina, was not around to see this, Aliajandra thought. His mother was her older sister. As different as two planets they were. But after Billy arrived they had become so much closer, and Aliajandra hoped that she had made up for the absence of a father figure in his life. Now, at fifty years of age, the age of concession, with his own family—his pretty wife, Elaine, and daughter Ariana—she felt content in the role she had played.

She stroked the invitation once again. And now she would have to endure the ceremonial as Billy embraced the affirmation. It wasn't his choice. Like a religion to cloak you, like a fur wrap on a chilly December morning, the affirmation was a statement but not really a choice; it was a duty event, decreed by law from the best of intentions. She could not fault him for approaching it like a real man. And as much as she hated it, it meant another reception, good food, good wine, and good company. How could she complain?

In the backyard, canopies had been erected to shield the eighty guests from the relentless summer sun. The chairs had been placed to afford each guest the best view, with a small handful of immediate family cloistered closer. They would sit in one corner of the elevated decking that would serve for the ceremony itself. As with most ceremonials, the aim was a personalized service, participation rather than merely an observance.

Even the minister presiding was a participant, Juliana Morgana from the Silent Sanctuary Church on Bishop Street, the daughter of the minister who had married Billy and Elaine thirty years earlier.

Billy fumbled with his bow tie. He was dressed in the same gray tuxedo that Elaine's father had worn at his affirmation some ten years earlier. He struggled to push unwarranted thoughts from his mind and concentrated instead on the arriving guests.

Georgianna hobbled in. At ninety she was the eldest of the trio of sisters, of which his mother had been one. Georgianna, forever theatrical, had applied an excess of lipstick and attempted to balance it by smearing her lips together. With her wide eyes, she looked a lot like Bette Davis in her later years; an imposing albeit scary figure, and one almost expected her to draw out a cigarette and inhale mercilessly. Instead, she hobbled over to Billy and pinched his cheek.

"Naughty boy," she said in a hoarse voice. "You never call me."

Billy was embarrassed. "Auntie Gee, you look lovely."

She turned her cheek for him to kiss and as his ear came close, she whispered, "Liar." He smiled. He could smell lilac water on her cold skin.

"Gigi, don't hurt the boy," Aliajandra interrupted. "He's the only nephew we have."

"Darling Ali," Georgianna said. "You're still with us, how lovely."

The two offered cheeks but neither kissed.

"And you don't look a day past one hundred," Aliajandra offered with a smile.

Georgianna took Ali's hand in her own and squeezed it affectionately. "That you'll look so good, darling sister. That you'll fare half as well as I, I can only hope for you."

Billy smiled. He had grown up with the two sisters always competing. It made him feel at home, free of pretension and facades. Here, now, his family held true. Perhaps, he pondered, this was the most significant moment of his life.

"I love you both very much," he told them. "Don't ever change."

Aliajandra laughed. "Ha. Little chance of that, my boy."

"We have to have the photographer shoot the three of us."

"I always tried to fill in for your mother, dear boy," Georgianna said. Aliajandra flashed her a dirty look. "All right, *we* all tried," she corrected herself. "We think of you as our own."

"I know," Billy said. "And you couldn't have done a better job."

"Your mother would have been proud."

Billy took both their hands in his own. "I am a lucky man."

Aliajandra took his face in her hands. "I just need to know one thing, Billy. That this is what you want, like this. I need to know you and Elaine are sure."

"Elaine and I have gone over this a thousand times. After thirty years of marriage, we're both in agreement that I have to do this. Besides, it's not like I really have a choice, is it?"

Aliajandra lowered her hands. Nodded. "Then I am here to help you in whatever way you need me to be," she said, ignoring his response.

"Thank you."

Upstairs Elaine tried focusing on her makeup. Her hands were trembling. She lowered the mascara and took a breath, then resumed. In the mirror she could see Ariana sitting on the bed, crying silently. At eighteen, Ariana was a pretty girl with dark hair and serious eyes.

Elaine put down the makeup and sat next to her, put her arm around her, pulled her closer, and then embraced her holding her tightly. Ariana was sobbing, her body heaving with each sob. Elaine just held her tightly, and rocked her gently before pulling back and stroking her hair.

"Your father and I have been married for thirty years. I know him well. Be happy for him. He needs that from you."

Ariana nodded, wiped tears from her eyes, and forced a smile for her mother. Elaine went back to the mirror and for a moment stared at her own reflection. Empty words, she pondered?

"It wasn't like this when your father and I got married," she continued. "We eloped to Vegas, but somehow my parents found out and called your grandmother, and the three of them flew out to Vegas, and just as your daddy and I were about to exchange vows, in they burst, panting, trying to stop us."

Elaine tied up her hair with a bow. "Daddy, I said, I love him. And your daddy said, 'Please Mr. Bancroft, you know I love Elaine very much. I just couldn't live without her.' Well, my parents already liked your father, and they just had nothing to say."

Ariana moved in closer. "So what happened?"

Elaine smiled. "We were married, and the three of them were our witnesses."

"That's neat, mom."

"Yeah," Elaine sighed. "Neat." But she was already feeling the tears forming in her own eyes. This here now was a stupid ritual and a stupid law, she thought, wanting to shout it out so that everyone could hear.

"Why does he have to do this?" Ariana finally asked. "Everyone says that it is the law, but it makes no sense that only men get to do this. What happened to equal rights?"

"Equal rights," Elaine blurted out. "You're right. It is stupid. Some bureaucrat's idea to control population and war, I suppose."

Downstairs Aliajandra cornered Georgianna after Billy had gone to find the photographer.

"Sister, we cannot allow this. Not for Billy."

"You just told the boy we would support his decision," Georgianna protested. "We're not?"

"Oh for God's sake, Gee, can you look me in the eye and tell me that you agree with this?"

Georgianna sipped at her drink. "Stupid or not, it is the law. At age 50 every male undergoes the Ceremonial for the good of the society," Georgianna started reciting the public service messages that always flashed on the TV. "Help save our planet from the ravages of overpopulation and warfare. Don't you remember what it was like before?"

Aliajandra laughed at the silly recital. "You have it memorized. Well, I suppose we all do. It's not like they do not show it enough on the telly. And what do we have to show for it? A world full of old women."

She placed her empty glass on the tray of a passing waiter and grabbed a full one, quickly taking a large swig.

"There is another way," she added. "Do you know that Elaine is upstairs in tears? And why wouldn't she be? Thirty years of marriage about to end because some fat politician passed a law."

"That fat politician was my husband," Georgianna reminded her. "He was trying to make a difference. Our world is dying, you know. Too many people and not enough resources. He managed to buy us some time." She wiped the tears from her eye with a crumpled piece of Kleenex she pulled from a sleeve, then stuffed it back in, again.

"Georgianna, you and I know that Bertie was a sexist ass. He treated you badly; heck he treated everyone badly and the only reason he made a law requiring men to die, but not women, was because he got paid from a corporation to get it through. Women outlive men as a rule. It should have been universal, if at all, or even the other way around. I do not want to outlive Billy."

"Found the photographer," Billy said, firmly grabbing the arm of the hired recorder. "The three of us, please," he instructed.

"By the lilies," Aliajandra told the man, grabbing her sister's arm and placing Billy's through it. Then she dabbed a napkin with some water from the table and patted down Billy's hair, as though he were a child just come in from playing outside.

"You are too much, Aunt Ali," he told her, taking the napkin from her and putting it aside. Gently he kissed her on the cheek and put her arm through his. "Our last picture together. It better be good."

The photographer adjusted his position.

"Can you see the lilies?" Aliajandra asked.

"Yes, ma'am. They are very prominent.," the photographer informed her.

In the background, a chime announced the start of the Ceremonial. Quickly the photo was taken.

"Go tend to your wife," Aliajandra told Billy. "She needs you."

Billy stood back and looked at them, one last look at the two women who were so important in his life. "Thank you, both," he said. "I love you both very much."

Immediately Georgianna erupted in tears. Aliajandra waved Billy away. "We love you, too, dear. Go tend to Elaine. Gee will be fine, won't you, dear?"

Georgianna had the ragged Kleenex again and nodded without looking at Billy. The truth was that Aliajandra had been right about Bertie, and because of Bertie, this horrible event was about to take place.

Billy nodded and quickly dashed up the stairwell.

"Listen to me," Aliajandra said. "The law is not infallible."

Georgianna looked up at her through swollen eyes. "Whatever do you mean?"

"You'll see. Let's get our seats. We have VIP status, you know."

Elaine was ready. Ariana held her hand as Billy approached.

"Daddy," Ariana whispered, letting go and grabbing her father, holding him close.

"It'll be alright, sweetheart," he tried to say assuringly, but his voice wavered. The thought of never seeing his wife and daughter again weighed heavily. And as much as everyone had considered him stoic about fulfilling this mandate of law, the truth was that he was scared, scared enough to have considered fleeing with his family.

He could have tried escaping past the border patrols and into Canada or Mexico, disappearing into the mountains somewhere and live out his life as a fugitive. At least they would have been together. At least he could have spared them the pain of this loss. The fact that he knew few fugitives who had succeeded bothered him more. Caught, his wife and daughter would be branded criminals and sent to a penal colony for helping him avoid his duty.

No, it won't be alright, he thought. But what choice do

I have? He kissed Ariana lightly on her forehead and reached for Elaine's hand. Tears were brimming, and he fought to hold them back. "I know you will remember only the good times," he told them. "I want you to be happy. I would be pained to learn that this resulted in the rest of your life being sad. I'm doing this for our family. I'm doing this so Ariana can grow up and become somebody important, maybe even find a solution to the problems in our world." He broke his hold to wipe at his eyes. "So please," he quietly resumed, "think only good thoughts and know how much I love you both."

"Oh, daddy," Ariana whimpered."I love you so much."

They could hear the music from downstairs and knew that the time had come.

"Ready?" Billy asked. Holding both their hands, they started down the stairs.

The invited watched from their seats. As Elaine and Billy came into view, the crowd erupted in applause.

"Just beautiful," someone said.

Billy led Elaine and Ariana to their seats on the platform where he would be processed.

Juliana Morgana waited, motioned for the women to sit, and then approached the microphone.

"Beloved family and guests. What can I say that you don't already know? We are gathered here to witness and behold the Ceremonial of Billy Paxler." She paused to look down, considering with care the words she would speak. "I performed the marriage ceremony of Billy and Elaine. I blessed the birth of their daughter, Ariana. I shared in the events of their lives, as they grew ever closer to this day, which we knew would come, as it does for all men."

The audience applauded.

"Billy," Juliana said, "has chosen to speak some words before the Ceremonial." She gestured for Billy to take his place at the microphone.

"Life passes too fast," he said. "It seems so short a time ago that I first stared into the eyes of this beautiful woman." He turned to point at Elaine. "The love of my life. The mother of my beautiful daughter. How could there not be love?"

From the front row of the audience, the two aunts watched. Aliajandra shook her head.

"Not fair," she muttered. Someone behind her shushed her.

"I lost my parents young," Billy continued. "I was fortunate to have two wonderful aunts who raised me as though I was their own. Auntie Ali and Auntie Gee, how do I say how much I owe you for a life filled with love?

Georgianna was dabbing her eyes. She looked at her sister, and each understood. Aliajandra stood. "I must be heard. My sister and I have no end of love for our Billy. While the passing of his mother grieved us both, that pain was more than overshadowed by the joy Billy brought to us. As parents, we could not be more proud.

The audience applauded.

Georgianna then stood, adjusted her dress, and her pearl necklace, and straightened her neck. "As you know, my beloved husband, Roberto Patrice, Head Justice for our nation-state, proposed and brought into law the Ceremonial. Despite less than flattering things that have been said, my husband was a great man and a great senator."

The audience applauded again.

"Thank you," Georgianna said. "It was his wish that our world would survive, that our population would not consume us under the weight of scarcity, poverty, famine and death. As a civilized man, he knew that we needed a civilized solution. And so he created the Ceremonial, a measure of a man's life, a tribute, an honor, and a final farewell, that, as any good provider, each man could make a final sacrifice for his family, to ensure their survival, and the survival of our society. I cannot fault him for that."

Georgianna moved forward toward Billy and Elaine.

"This year, on my birthday in two months, I will be seventy-five years old. My husband is long dead. I am alone, except for my sister, Aliajandra. I have lived a full life."

Aliajandra called out. "We have both lived a full life."

Julianna sensed that this was breaking from the program. Moving toward Georgianna, she reached out to embrace her, cutting off any further words that would emerge. At least, that was her hope.

"I am exercising my rights as a citizen," Aliajandra shouted out. "I call for an end to the Ceremonial. It is a violation of our Constitutional rights."

"Boo," someone yelled out. "You challenge it because it is your nephew."

Aliajandra turned in fury. "Who dares suggest that? Which one of you cowardly, sniveling masses believes that I, Alejandra Maria Velotte would violate the law? I dare you to stand up to me?"

No one responded.

Georgianna moved next to her sister.

"Darling Billy," Aliajandra said, staring directly at him. "As one of your aunts, your direct blood, my sister and I absolve you of the Ceremonial, under Article Eighteen, Section . . ." she turned to Georgianna, "what is the section, for God's sake? You know this stuff. . . ."

"Twenty-four," Georgianna jumped in. "Section twenty-four states that in lieu of a Ceremonial, a blood relative may substitute in place of the initiate."

Aliajandra turned to the audience, indignant. "I hereby offer myself in substitution of Billy."

Juliana was aghast. "You can't do that? This is Billy's day, and you are ruining it for him."

Aliajandra would hear nothing of it. "Don't be silly," she snapped at Juliana. "I am giving my nephew the greatest gift a parent could give; a long life with his wife and child."

"She is correct," Georgianna said. "That is a part of the statute, even though most people selfishly never exercise it." She motioned to the audience. "How many of you have seen your husbands go off to the Ceremonial and done nothing to stop it?" She turned back to Aliajandra. "Sister, I take back every mean thing I ever said about you. You are the noblest person I know."

Aliajandra grinned. It was noble, and she knew it.

"However," Georgianna said, "I cannot allow you to do so alone. I hereby forfeit my life as well. Since my sister has covered the debt for Billy's life, I hereby bequeath my life for a future Ceremonial, to be determined by my nephew, Billy. Billy, will you agree to this?"

Billy was already moving toward them both, tears staining his face that he carelessly wiped. "You can't do this. It's my job to do this."

Aliajandra was the first to grab him. "Ssssh," she said. "Please, dear boy, take this gift. Please, don't argue. I cannot live to see Elaine live a life without the man she loves. I cannot live to see your daughter miss her father every day of her life. Please. . . ."

Billy was sobbing uncontrollably. Georgianna moved closer, and the three of them held each other.

"It's a good choice, Billy," Georgianna told him. "It is a

very good choice. What greater gift can a parent give their child than one of life?"

"I don't deserve this," Billy said between sobs.

Aliajandra held his face in her hands and made him look her in the eyes. "You have to swear that you will do as Gee asked. Yes? Yes?" Billy nodded. "And for me, you will devote your life to ending this stupid law. There has got to be a better way. You must be the one to find it. Promise me? Honor my life with that promise?"

"I promise," Billy told her, wiping his tears. "Thank you. I love you both so much."

"We know, dear boy," Georgianna told him.

"We always knew," Aliajandra said. She kissed him on the cheek, then quickly broke her grip on him, moving to the Ceremonial stage, giving Elaine and Ariana a hug, and pushing them all toward the audience seats. "Go be with your daddy, child," she said. Ariana could barely compose herself. Quickly she ran to her father and threw herself at him, holding him tightly.

Georgianna walked after her sister, not looking back. She knew that she could not face looking at Billy. She knew that this was the right thing to do.

Juliana Morgana stood in shock. She had overseen almost a hundred Ceremonials, and none had ended like this.

"Well," she said, clearing her throat and facing the audience. "This will have to be done one after the other.

I'm afraid we are not prepared for two simultaneous Ceremonials."

"Don't worry about it, dear," Georgianna told her. "Two is better than one."

"I go first," Aliajandra said. "Beauty before age, Gee." She sat on the table edge with Georgianna by her side. "You have always been the best sister. I know we were always competitive, but you know how much I have always loved you, don't you?"

"I know," Georgianna said. "Why do you think I have to leave with you? It's always been the two of us."

"We did a good thing," Aliajandra said.

"No," Georgianna corrected her. "We did a grand thing. Father would be very proud of us."

"Yes, he would," Aliajandra said. "Do you believe we will see him again? You know, on the other side?"

Georgianna smiled and nodded. Beside the table, a vase with lilies offered a stark contrast to what would happen. Georgianna pulled two lilies from the vase and handed one to her sister. "You always loved lilies. See you on the other side, sister." She leaned in and kissed her on the cheek, then stepped back so the technicians could do their work.

"The Lord hath given us life," Juliana said loudly so all could hear. "From the darkness, He giveth life and called upon us to exercise our own agency with that we hath received. Aliajandra Marie, of your own choice, have you willingly chosen to give up unto your Father in Heaven, the spirit which you were given?"

"Yes," Aliajandra said. "Can we get on with this, please?"

The technicians pulled up each sleeve gently, wiped the spot where the needle would be inserted, and gingerly broke the ivory skin of both arms at the elbow crease, where the vein stood firm. Aliajandra winced briefly. The technicians taped the line in place and nodded their readiness to Juliana.

"By the power invested in me, and in the name of our Father in Heaven, we commend your spirit so that others may live. We do so willingly, peacefully, and with the love He has shown to us. May He lead your light. I say this in His name. Blessed be His name."

The audience parroted. "Blessed be His name."

Juliana nodded and the technician opened the line, allowing the chemicals to flow freely into the veins. Aliajandra breathed in deeply, allowing herself to fully absorb the flavor of the air, the richness of her lungs filling, and the fragrance of the lily by her side. She turned to look at her sister as the chemicals took hold, at first blurring her vision before reducing her senses to a small sphere before blackness took hold. "Here I go . . . ," she whispered, but the words never came out.

The technician listened for a heartbeat, but there was none. The audience applauded, and offered a standing ovation for the life well lived, before sitting down again.

Carefully, Aliajandra's body was moved to an adjacent table. After Georgianna, this would be the public viewing, a final chance to say goodbyes. Georgianna brushed her hand against her sister's cheek. It was already cold. She worked up the courage to look up at Billy. He was crying uncontrollably, held close by Elaine and Ariana. Georgianna smiled at him and blew him a kiss.

As soon as the body was removed, Georgianna lay down in the same spot that her sister had occupied and allowed the technicians to insert the feed lines and waited for the preamble, yet again.

"I don't know what to say," Juliana said. "Lord, you hath taken from us one of two sisters as tokens of another life. Before you lies the heart of both, Georgianna Louise, daughter of Frederick Hausser. I beg you to grace these sisters with thy blessings for the sacrifice they have made today." Juliana turned toward Georgianna, and leaned in closer. "Bless you," she whispered, tears forming in her eyes.

Georgianna motioned for her to come closer. With Juliana's ear close by, Georgianna whispered, "Get on with it."

Juliana nodded to the technicians who opened the flow valve. Georgianna stared at the sky. How pretty it looked. And then it all brightened up, and she knew that she was seeing the other side and her sister there with Billy's mother and their father. With a final breath, she smiled.

Billy stood before the technicians pronounced. Loudly he began to clap his hands. Elaine and Ariana quickly joined in, and then the audience as a whole. He wiped his eyes, walked over to his aunts, and stood between them. He held each hand and looked at the audience.

"I hereby promise that I will devote my life to bring to an end this act of loss, this waste of life, this farce that many die so few can live."

The audience began to applaud. The waiters were already bringing the champagne. Billy summoned one to him and took a glass, holding it high.

"A toast," he shouted out. "I celebrate the lives of my three mothers, Jacquelina, Aliajandra and Georgianna. May they live forever. God knows that I miss them."

"Hear, hear," the crowd chanted.

CHAPTER TEN
AFTER THE LEAVES

"I MISS the leaves on the trees," Sam said. He was the first to speak, mostly bothered by the unbearable stillness after the family awoke. "You never really appreciate things like that until afterwards."

"Melly was in the lead," Dad said, "her hair long like a waterfall—gosh, do you remember how much she would brush it every day? I used to worry that it would all fall out and she'd wind up bald like me."

Kari giggled at the image, then stopped as she remembered. "It's not fair, daddy."

"It's not fair," Dad said, kissing her lightly on the forehead. "But it is real, sweetheart. Always remember the real."

And Kari played the 'real' back again, the explosions, the smoke, thick and biting at the throat, the air shrouded with dust and chemicals and burning at the eyes, and the screaming—seemingly endless screaming like some twisted chorus. And somehow she had managed to fall asleep, and by the time she awoke, the 'real' was still there except for the screaming that had been lost.

"Stop being such a baby," Melly had snapped at her, mascara running down her face and mingled with ash and soot. Her eyes had dark red spider veins and her eyebrows had been singed, stubby black hair sticking straight up with small blackened blobs at the end. Kari remembered staring at it wanting to touch the ends.

"Lucky for us we had the cabin," Dad said, "so we knew where to go. But of course, the roads were broken, and even if they were intact, the cars would have blocked the way. Good thing we always went on weekend hikes. Good thing we knew what to do or we'd be lost like the rest of them. When I was a boy, your grandpa would tell me that there were only two types of people in the world . . . ."

Kari jumped in. "Smart people or dead people."

"Exactly. I guess we were the smart people."

"Was Melly not smart?"

Dad thought on this, rubbed the stubble on his face, and considered his answer. His eyes were swollen, red veins like tree roots spread across the whites. "Melly was smart," he finally said. "She was just unlucky."

Kari left it at that, although she wanted to say that luck seemed irrelevant now that the leaves had fallen.

"But *you* are very smart," Dad told her. "And Sam, too."

"And Mommy would have been smart, also."

Dad smiled. "Mommy was the smartest of all of us."

"I miss her every day," Kari said.

"Every day," Dad whispered. "Think you can sleep?"

Kari shrugged. "Can Sam finish the story, tonight?"

Dad kissed her again and went to get Sam. Kari stared at her room while she waited, her eyes tracing shapes in the ceiling until they drifted to her shortwave radio in the corner. It was too early to talk with Stephanie. Stephanie was also smart, maybe even smarter than the rest of them since she was alone now. But they could only talk for a short time otherwise the generator would run out of gas faster. Ten minutes was all she was allowed. Ten minutes to say the world of words. Ten minutes to hug and hold and cry. She wished they could scoop up Stephanie and bring her to their cabin, but there was no way. Kari knew she would never meet Stephanie.

"Hey squirt," Sam said, breaking her thoughts. "My turn, Dad said."

Kari smiled at him. "I love you, Sammy," she said."Do you know that?"

Sam nodded. "Always did." He sat down on the bed. "Where'd Dad stop at?"

"Smart people . . . ."

"Oh, that! Okay. Well, we make it to the cabin even though it took us days and days. Melly was sick then, and Dad had to carry her for the last part, which is why Dads are always the strongest of all.

And then finally we got here."

"I used to hate coming here," Kari said. "I hated hiking. It was so boring."

"Yeah, but then Dad let you have his old shortwave and you liked it after that."

Kari shifted on the bed. "The radio is so cool. Every kid should have one."

"Maybe one day it'll be a law that every kid has to have a shortwave," Sam told her.

"So after we got to the cabin," Kari said, "you and Daddy went to check on the supplies that we had left last summer."

"Exactly. Dad was afraid that we had not stocked up as we should have and that there might not have been enough food."

"And no one else had broken in."

"Dad had his shotgun by his side and we walked around the outside first, looking for footprints, but there weren't any." Sam brushed his long hair back over his head. "Dad told you to see who was on the shortwave . . . ."

". . . and that was when I found Stephanie," Kari interrupted. "She was all alone over there."

"Well, New Zealand is . . . ." He stopped and looked down at the wooden planks of the floor, and the dust that covered it. He wanted to just go to sleep and not have to think about it anymore but Dad had said that they'd sleep soon enough and needed to be alert for now. "It's almost time to talk to Stephanie, isn't it?"

"I hope so," Kari said. "But you'll have to carry me over there—I don't want to fall again."

From outside Dad started up the generator.

Gently Sam pulled the covers back and lifted Kari effortlessly. Sam was the strongest of all of them, she told herself. Nothing could knock him down.

He put her down on the chair and pushed it closer, then leaned over to plug in the shortwave radio. Kari waited for it to come alive before slowly turning up the volume and adjusting the frequency. Dad walked in behind them and put his hand on Sam's neck and pulled him closer, kissing him on the top of his head. Silence.

"November Seven, Pesky Montana Skunk. This is Kari. Stephanie, can you read me?"

Silence. Dad's hand gripped tighter.

"November Seven, Pesky Montana Skunk. This is Kari. Stephanie, can you read me?"

Kari looked back at them. She was already thinking the worst.

"Try again, honey," Dad told her.

"November Seven, Pesky Montana Skunk. This is Kari. Stephanie, can you read me?"

Silence.

"Daddy, what if something happened to her? What if she didn't make it?"

Dad just stood there, their eyes locked. It wasn't too much to ask for. Just a little more time. His little girl deserved that much and he wanted nothing for himself.

The room suddenly erupted with static and a child's voice said, "Kilo Bravo Three Helo Tango Sam. This is Stephanie. Hi Kari. I'm so glad to hear your voice."

And the three of them began to laugh hard and deep and their laughter filled the cabin with life.

BONUS STORY: A LIMITED POINT OF VIEW

Grandy turned from the window where only moments before he had been staring hypnotically out at the great void between it and the ground some two miles below. The sensation of power was incredible, almost overwhelming. It was as though there existed within the empty space some kind of unseen power just waiting to be used, pulling him out and down.

It had been another long day, as they all were, and he felt a certain sense of relief at the sight of the twin suns gracefully setting behind the farthest building. The view from the windows was all the same, a cluster of pencil-like structures, seemingly an arm's reach apart. Depending on how high up you were, and in which building, would determine the amount of unobstructed view you would receive.

The buildings were designed on the March Efficiency Scale, a scale designed individually for each building. And it was Frederik March himself who allocated the height of the building for the prospective company concerned. The higher up you worked, the more important your position. The aim would be to reach the Penthouse, something attained with some difficulty as one would have to wait for the previous occupant (also the company president) to either retire, have a nervous breakdown, or die.

Consequently, the higher up you went, the longer the number of hours you would have to put in. The lower levels generally worked a four-hour day. The mid-levels a seven to ten-hour day, and the upper levels anywhere from ten to sixteen hours a day—based on the Government Medical Board decision that humans required only seven hours of rest and one hour for meals. Those building owners never had any "spare" time. There was no need. If it wasn't for the good of the company then it would be eliminated from the daily ritual.

Grandy was only two levels from the top. He worked a sixteen-hour day before returning home to his wife and three children. He would leave at eight in the evening, arriving home just in time for dinner. He would sit down for five minutes, have a drink, eat and then spend an hour with the children. They would go to bed. His wife would sit beside him. Then they'd make love and they would go to sleep. He would be awake at three in the morning and off to work at three-twenty, arriving for the start of the four o'clock shift. And so it would go on.

Each year the days seemed longer. His paycheck would increase, but then so too would taxes. And he was only two levels from the top. Two levels from the luxurious offices of Travis Eastman, owner of the (now) Eastman Building.

He knew Eastman quite well. When he joined the company, known then as the Winfield Building, Eastman was on the third level. Grandy would sneak up in his spare time to watch the higher offices at work, wanting desperately to reach the top. Now he was two levels away. Eastman was at the top. And Eastman was ill. Grandy wanted the top floor and the only thing between him and Eastman's level was Johnson.

He disliked Johnson. The man arrived straight into the thirtieth position. He had presented a letter to the Employment Board, a letter signed by some important person—Grandy never found out who—and overtook everyone. No one liked him. No one except Eastman. He never took a position away from Eastman.

Grandy hoped that Eastman would soon die. He knew it was a nasty thought to wish someone dead like that, so easily and so cruelly. But that was what he wanted. Above all else, he wanted Eastman dead.

He had thought about killing him secretly. He was not

sure whether he could or not, but he knew one thing; the day of Eastman's death would be a happy one for the building. Everyone would automatically advance up one level.

The suns had just set and he would soon be home in a few hours. It had been a long day, calculating stocks, buying and selling for the old man upstairs. It had been a long day just for Grandy who wanted at this moment nothing more than to go home and make love to his wife. But he would have to wait. He always had to wait. It was all a matter of patience and timing.

He turned from the window and returned to his desk. It was a large desk with one of those large comfortable swivel chairs which executives always enjoyed. And he sat down. There were books shelved neatly against one wall and a small mobile bar, his own. To one side there was a closet and beyond that a door leading to a private shower cubicle.

He placed his feet up on the desk and leaned back in the chair. He should have been working. He had stacks of paperwork to complete, assess and sign. That was all he really did, approve someone else's work. The whole building ran on the work done by the lower levels. All the bosses had to do was sign. He didn't feel like signing anything more today.

The phone rang. He picked it up.

"Grandy."

"This is Eastman. I need to see you for about ten minutes. Come up will you?"

"Sure," Grandy replied, putting down the phone and standing. He reached behind him for his jacket and carelessly put it on. Then he walked out towards the aerovator. He had to wait twenty seconds for the first available one, then stepped in and said, "Penthouse". The aerovator accelerated upwards. He arrived, the doors opened and he stepped out.

Two security guards greeted him at the door, gun barrels crossed until they had identified him.

"I have an appointment," he told them. They obliged and shifted out of his way. He walked into the Eastman Offices. Eastman's secretary looked up at him and smiled, then nodded and looked back down. He walked past her and into Eastman's office.

"Ah, Grandy," Eastman said, standing and motioning him to a seat. Grandy sat with one leg crossed over the other. "I called you up here because I have something to tell you. My doctor has told me that I will likely have a fatal heart attack very soon, because of the ones I've had recently. I thought you ought to know that the prognosis isn't good. I don't think that I will be around for much longer."

Grandy listened. It would have been ridiculous to even suggest that he take some time off to try and recover. It was unheard of. No one wanted that. The whole system warranted his being there. He made all the decisions. To leave would simply incite a coup from a lower subordinate seeking power. Eastman would never risk it.

"I understand," Grandy said. "But why tell me? It's Johnson who will inherit next."

"Yes, yes, I know that," the old man snapped, "I just wanted you to know. We've been in this building a long time, you and I."

“We have," Grandy replied, “and you've been the owner for most of that time.”

"You think I should be out of here now, don't you?”

"What I think has little bearing, sir," Grandy answered.

"Yes, I guess it does at that," Eastman told him, “It's just that I think Johnson should *not* be next, that's all. It was one thing for him to join us late, but not to inherit until it was his turn. It’s wrong.”

"But there's nothing you can do about it now. You accepted him in at level thirty. He has his rights. "

"I know . . . ," Eastman said. “I had no choice. I just wanted you to know that I don't approve. I would be very . . . glad . . . to see . . . something happens to him and to see you in charge instead,” he said, emphasizing each word.

"Thank you, sir. I take that as a compliment," Grandy said.

"It was meant to be Mr. Grandy. It was meant to be. "

Grandy left the office pondering Eastman's remark. Was it a hint to him that he should do something? Did he want to? It would be difficult. Johnson was a relatively young man, still in his fifties. He was two years younger than Grandy—obviously a late starter in life—aided by his instant elevation to the thirtieth level. He had no wife or kids. Just ambition.

But worse, he could hold the Penthouse for another twenty years, depending, of course, on how his health held up. And that would deprive Grandy of the presidency he felt that he deserved—that he had earned.

At seven-fifty-nine that evening, Grandy put back on his jacket and reached for his briefcase. And at eight exactly he left his office for the aerovator. There was no waiting time. His level would be the only departure at that hour.

He entered it and waited for a moment before the doors closed and the unit plunged the two-mile drop to street level. As he stepped out of the aerovator someone called out to him, "Goodnight Mr. Grandy."

He turned. It had been his secretary. He nodded and walked on. When he reached home, the door was slightly ajar. He pushed it open and walked in. He could smell dinner from where he stood, wafting in waves from the kitchen.

"Hi, honey," came a shrill voice from some other part of the house. Then his wife appeared from around the corner holding a handful of cutlery. He leaned forward slightly and kissed her.

"Hi, how was work ?"

"Long as usual. What's for dinner?"

"A roast. It'll be ready in a minute."

"Where're the kids?"

"Oh, my mother has them sleeping over. She thought we might enjoy the peace and quiet.

"Hmmm," Grandy hummed, hugging her tightly, pressing himself against her.

"Can't you wait until after dinner?" she asked, laughing at his lack of subtlety. Grandy shook his head, *no*.

"Well you'd better," she added, pulling away, "I've slaved over that roast so you'd better appreciate it first."

During dinner, he wondered whether he would tell her about his meeting with Eastman. He had never lied to her before. Nor had he kept anything from her. She always had approved of anything he had done, knowing that it was for all of them that he did it. But he didn't know what she'd think of his latest idea.

"Eastman called me up today," he finally said.

"Oh," she looked up, placing her fork down. "What for ?"

"He's had two heart attacks last week, doesn't think he'll be around too long. "

"That's wonderful honey," she replied, smiling and leaning over to kiss him.

"Yeah, but it means Johnson will be number one."

"Well, you knew that would happen."

"The only trouble is he's younger than I am. I'd lose out completely. I'll never get to the Penthouse."

"I know honey . . . and I'm sorry," she said, trying to console him, "but you can never tell. He might have a nervous breakdown. It is quite common, isn't it? Many execs can't handle the pressure."

"Sure, but there are no guarantees. He's fairly strong."

She looked at him, then kissed him again. Then she collected the dishes and placed them in the washer. Grandy moved to the couch. She joined him. He reached for her and drew her toward him, kissing her.

"I love you," she whispered to him. Then they went to the bedroom and made love.

The next morning he arrived at his office at four o'clock. A cup of coffee had already been placed on his desk by his secretary. It was something she had always done, something not required in her services to him. He thought for a moment that it was a good system. She would ascend with him after Eastman's death. Her life would be easier after that.

She had once walked into his office after two weeks of employment and undressed before him. When he asked her why she had told him that a few of her previous bosses had expected her to sleep with them. He was shocked. He had never even contemplated the idea. He assured her that she would not have to under his employment.

He had gone home that night and told his wife about it. She had laughed. He wasn't quite sure why she had laughed. Either she had found it funny or felt reassured that her husband wasn't fooling around. But then he rarely had time to fool around.

He sat down and sipped on the coffee. The intercom buzzed and he answered. It was his secretary with some papers for him to sign. He told her to come in.

"Janice," he began, "I don't know if I've told you this, but your coffee is very much appreciated."

"Thank you, sir," she replied, slightly embarrassed. She handed him the papers and then left. He glanced at them and then flipped them onto the table. He would tend to them later. There were more pressing matters with which to tend.

He stood up and began to pace the office. He knew what he had to do, not only for himself but for his wife and kids as well. He had thought about it since the meeting with Eastman. He had thought about it through dinner with his wife, and even while they made love. And last night he had even dreamed the scenario. He had to be the next president of the company.

At twelve-eleven he left his office and walked to the stairs, up to Johnson's office. He knew his secretary would be out; all secretaries were out, all having the same lunch hour. He walked through the outer office and then knocked on Johnson's door.

"Come in."

He entered. Johnson was seated behind his desk scribbling out something. He glanced up quickly.

"Oh, it's you Grandy. Sit down Be right with you. "

Grandy walked around the desk to the window and gazed out for a moment. Then he reached into his jacket pocket and withdrew the small club he had made from a solid bronze trophy on his desk, raised it high and slammed it down across Johnson's neck as hard as he could. Johnson let out a short grunt and fell flat across the table, blood starting to swell down his back.

Grandy rolled him out of the way then, pulling up the guest chair, sat by the typewriter and, from his drawer, withdrew a pre-signed blank letterhead. Johnson was quite lazy about that sort of thing, allowing his secretary to fill in letters based on his verbal instructions to her, not having to wait for his signature. Grandy began to type:

To whom it may concern. I have had enough of all this. I can't go on. The pain and the headaches are not worth the small successes of working in Eastman's Building. I have decided to end it. Forgive me for my selfishness.

The signature made it official.

Grandy folded it quickly and stuffed it into an envelope, leaving it atop Johnson's desk. He lifted the guest chair he was sitting on and used it to smash the window. There was a *whoosh* sound as the air pressure equalized, and he watched the glass shards falling.

Then he lifted Johnson's body and carried it to the gaping hole, and let it fall. He watched for a moment as the body seemed almost to sail, then arms and legs flapping as the body spiraled in its rapid descent.

He left, carefully wiping his prints from the typewriter on the way out. And he returned to his office. Lunch was almost over. He ducked into the stairwell as he heard the aerovator chime.

As he walked into his office, he heard the screams from Johnson's secretary, short, piercing bursts. Janice also walked in, and Grandy gave her a quizzical look.

"Better go see what that's about," he told Janice. But he already knew that Johnson's secretary had seen the smashed window, looked out at the drop miles below, the note on the desk, and figured it out.

While Johnson lived, she had a job, but now that he was dead, she had nothing. She would have to find new employment or start again at the bottom. Those were the rules. There was nothing worse than trying to find a job when your last boss killed himself.

Grandy flinched. He flinched because he knew that it was all beginning to fall into place for him. He would not have long to wait at all before Eastman would considerately pass on, the helm of the corporation now going to

Grandy. The building would be renamed the Grandy Building, a mark of respect for his position. He had waited for thirty-years for this moment. And even though he had aided in speeding the process along, he reveled in the anticipation he felt.

At two that afternoon, he was summoned back to Eastman's office where he sat down and waited for the old man to get off the phone.

"I suppose you heard about Johnson?" Eastman began. "He left this note on his desk." Eastman handed him the note that Grandy had typed. "It's a suicide note, but the investigators believe he was murdered."

"Murdered? Why?" Grandy asked in genuine disbelief. How could they have known? The body fell two miles down?

"Because he had every reason to live. He knew that I would be gone soon enough. "

"Then who?" Grandy asked, his palms now wet with sweat.

"You, Grandy. They suspect you." Eastman's eyes twinkled. He wanted to watch Grandy squirm a bit. God knows there were so few enjoyable moments left to him. "At least they thought that until I told them that I had killed him," Eastman finally said.

Grandy was in shock. "You . . . but why would you say that?"

"Because I wanted you in charge, not Johnson. And

because I have had a good long run and nothing to lose. You see, I remember things the way they were before the ascension system took over. If nothing else, I have at least secured the man I want to take over where I left off. So I told them that I killed him because I wanted you to follow me. I have nothing to lose. And they won't do a thing to you because it was my doing. Order has been preserved. I'm an old man with less than a week to live. They didn't even arrest me. They just gave me a summons to appear in court. If I am still alive."

"So the matter is closed then?" Grandy asked, surprised at the unexpected outcome; this was the man he had once contemplated murdering.

"To all intents and purposes, the matter is closed," Eastman said, then, holding out his hand, "Congratulations Grandy. You've earned it. Do me proud, will you?"

Grandy shook his hand. He didn't know what to say. In just this last minute, he had gained immense respect for the man. "Thank you, sir."

"Good luck," Eastman told him. Then Grandy left.

He wondered whether he should postpone moving into Johnson's office. There seemed to be little point in having to move twice when he could wait an extra week.

Back in his own office, Grandy picked up the phone and dialed home. His wife answered. "I thought you might like to know that you were right," he told her. He could feel his heart racing, and his skin drenched in perspiration.

"Right about what, honey?"

"About Johnson. He jumped out of the window this morning. Suicide."

"That's terrific news, honey. That's really wonderful. Is everything okay?"

"Yes," Grandy replied, "everything's fine now."

As he ended the call, he could feel the anticipation building within him. All those years of waiting, working upwards in this building, one slow level after another, new offices, new friends, and new views. And power . . . much more power each time.

And as he thought about all the changes, he remembered how he had first walked into the Winfield Building, as it was called back then when Paul Winfield was president; how he had sweated out the interview before the employment board as they asked him a million questions. He had answered truthfully, intent on working his way up. He remembered how Eastman had put in a good word for him, then two slots above him, until the day Johnson arrived.

Then he thought about the lonely hours he had put in, four in the morning till eight in the evening, looking forward to making love to his wife, seeing the kids, sleeping. It seemed so easy to just let it slide, to break down as he had made it look like Johnson had broken down. He wondered whether the body had landed in one piece. *It would be on the news tonight*, he thought.

Then he thought about the day Janice had walked into his office and removed her clothes and how he had been shocked, shocked only that it had been so unexpected. He remembered staring at her, tracing a line with his eyes along her body, pausing at her breasts, realizing that he had never before even stopped and imagined what they might have been like. To touch, caress, and explore, all within the privacy of his office where he could take his time. And he wondered why he had turned her down. It all seemed like such a long time ago.

He could already visualize the official announcement of Eastman's death next week, a short ceremonial prayer to send him off, and the order to elevate, with special congratulations to Joseph Grandy, the new President of the Grandy Building. A new sign would be erected in neon midway up the side of the immense tower for all to see, his measure of permanence, his recognition.

He reached into his pocket and dug out a handkerchief, frantically wiping his brow. His heart was pounding, and he felt slightly dizzy at the excitement.

"Control yourself," he whispered aloud. "Calm down."

He took a deep breath, then stood and walked to the bar and poured himself a whiskey. He swallowed it quickly, holding the glass to his lips for a moment longer, feeling the liquid burning at him from within.

Then he sat down again. He reached for the intercom and pressed the button marked 'speak.'

"Janice. Can you come in here, please!"

PLEASE HELP THE AUTHOR WITH A QUICK REVIEW

Thank you for reading this collection of short stories. I hope you enjoyed them.

As you know, getting traction for an author is not an easy task. In fact, reviews are the best way for others to discover this book.

I would like to ask you to take a few moments and submit a review so that others can read your honest opinion. It would mean a lot to me.

Thank you.

~William Gensburger

ALSO BY WILLIAM GENSBURGER

- Texas Dead Book 1
- Angle of Death Book 2
- American Dead Book 3
- The Texas Dead Trilogy.

www.ingramcontent.com/pod-product-compliance
Lightning Source LLC
Chambersburg PA
CBHW072008210726
48294CB00013B/1723
* 9 7 8 1 7 3 7 9 8 6 2 7 0 *